Granite
Stories

A Novel By
Vance Bennett

Little Owl Publishing
6155 Mountain View Drive
Winnemucca, Nevada, 89445

Memories light the corners of my mind
Misty water-colored memories of the way we were
Scattered pictures of the smiles we left behind
Smiles we gave to one another for the way we were.
Can it be that it was all so simple then
Or has time rewritten every line
If we had the chance to do it all again
Tell me, would we?
Could we?

Marvin Hamlisch (1973)

Prologue

"Go ahead, try it on for size. It won't hurt." That's probably what Smokey would tell you.

The year is 1977 and you are in your twenties again. You owe no one and no one owes you. You're just looking for a paycheck and a place to be.

You're traveling on that muddy, pot-holey, raggedy ass, piece of road we used to call the North Fork Highway in a battered old sedan with bald tires and seven dollars and twenty-seven cents in your pocket.

You're looking at what's left of that town; a town leftover from lifetimes past; a falling down town at the head of an emerald green meadow being covered with the first of a new winter's fresh snow.

This is a tale about that town.

This is also a tale about those of us that populated that town during the late nineteen seventies and early eighties.

This is a tale about Katy Gunn, Timothy O'Leary, Jim, Alice, and Cecil. Children born of the late nineteen forties and early fifties. A piece of what was loosely referred to as the "Working Class" back in those days. A piece of what was known by the demographic parceling of a generation called "Baby Boomers."

Then there was Thor, Smokey, Angelina, and Marshal Bud. Those that seemed like they had always been there. They were our elders, so to speak; the keepers of the local wisdom.

1

Then there was Sonny and his people. Hillbillies, for want of a better label. Those that migrated from the Blue Ridge Mountains in Virginia to the Blue Mountains of Eastern Oregon.

Most of this working man's ditty contains a lot of fiction, but it's not a total fabrication in any sense of the word.

The place is/was real. So were the people that charactered that place. I knew most of those people at one time or another.

What I did with a few characters in this narrative was to take pieces and parts from each of those people I knew back then and stir them around until they became the one personality that wrapped around them all.

Then there were those individuals I didn't need to. That's just who they were. I didn't even try and change the names because another name just wouldn't fit.

The Federal Writers' Project (FWP) was a United States federal government project created to provide jobs for out-of-work writers during the Great Depression. It was part of the Works Progress Administration (WPA), a New Deal program. (Wikipedia)

A gentleman named William C. Haight was a member of the FWP.

He was part of what was called the {*American Life Histories (Manuscripts from the Federal Writers Project, 1936 to 1940.)*} Basically, what William did was get in touch with people; people past generations– those from that place, but a different time – and conduct an interview.

I have grafted several of Mr. Haight's interviews – along with interviews conducted by others from that particular place and time – into this narrative. What I have endeavored is to give an inkling as to what life might have been like as the nineteenth was turning into the twentieth century.

One of those several people Mr. Haight interviews is a gentleman named Carle Hentz; a German immigrant and a teamster in that part of the world in the years around 1885 or so; in a world when transportation was a little different; transportation before the advent of the internal combustion engine.

Another of those interviewed by Mr. Haight was a German/American woman named Neil Niven. She was an eighteen-year-old "School Marm" in Granite, Oregon in and around the years of 1880 and 1890. William C. Haight referred to Mrs. Neil Niven, as elderly, literate, and "Rather Irascible."

I've tried to illustrate what life for us in the late nineteen seventies was like compared life back late eighteen hundreds.

And while I was at it I may have also stumbled onto the many ways those lives may have been the same.

"The Gold Dust Twins" isn't exactly part of the story. However, if you do decide to read this book you'll get the idea as to why it's there.

"William C. Dex" really isn't even a chapter. I guess you could call it a story of its own, albeit a brief one. The three characters, taken out of the 1880 Granite census roles, actually existed. I just rearranged them to suit my own purposes.

Many lyrics from a lot of tunes in here.

Some of those lyrics belong to folksongs from days long past, but most came from the late sixties, the seventies, and the early eighties. Think of those tunes as a sound track if you will, for you see, we were young, and that's the way we were.

Ghost towns along the highway
So many people used to call this place home
Ghost towns along the highway
I guess folks they're just bound to roam.

John Mellencamp (1981)

The Darkness

The darkness is total and complete. It won't do any good to sit and wait till your eyes adjust, because there is nothing for them to adjust too. You won't see the stars. You won't eventually see the outline of your hands, like on a moonless inky black night. All you'll see is just the black. All you'll see is the total absence of light; darkness complete, and overwhelming.

As you feel your way up and out, into the open air and the bright sunshine, your world becomes a very beautiful place. It kind of goes from an elongated two dimensions to three, if that makes any sense. It's no longer just a long black tube. Your world takes in a breath of clean fresh air and gets a whole lot bigger. It takes on a myriad number of colors. All well named: Earth Tones. There are a lot of different shades of green, and every subtle shade of brown

.

Timothy O'Leary July 2, 1978

Jim and I found that bit of script in the log book we kept around in the Dry to let the shift coming on know what was going on.

Timothy had tripped over an air hose down near the Face and broken his light. When he gathered is senses, and felt the broken lens on that light, he then realized his life was totally without light.

He had to feel is way along the Rib, hands out front, touching, feeling... a dark, black, inch at time. Sliding one foot out to feel for rock, then another foot forward, then another. He had to feel his way towards the comfort of day light and fresh air better than three-quarters a mile away.

5

Sometimes Timothy O'Leary's logbook writings could be rather profound.

The Gold Rush

Some say the first to find his way to what later became a town named Granite was a man named Harvey Robbins in a wagon pulled by eight head of oxen in 1862. Some say a man named A.G. Tabor took a pan and started washing the sand and loose gravel from one of those clear running streams and found a little gold, then a little more.

Not long after those that heard of Mr. Tabor's find began to populate that place and began moving the boulders in those streams around, trying to get to bedrock, finding more gold yet.

People from all over this world came looking for that gold. The Irish and the Scotts; the Germans and the Dutch; the Spaniards and the Chinese; departing the places of their birth, their homes, and their lives, to go to a place thousands of miles away to search for that gold.

They cast big nozzles called monitors and hooked those monitors to big pieces of hand riveted pipe. Then they plumbed that pipe into those mountain streams, and washed the sides of those very same mountains through the sluices they had built. They built ditches and wooden flumes long distances to where more gold might be found so they would have the water to power the wheels that drove the washing plants, the trommels and arrastra.

When the placer gold began to dwindle, they hauled in heavy electric generators with teams of often more than twenty mules. Then they diverted those very same streams through those generators for the power to drive the mills that crushed the rock and processed the ore that came out of the tunnels, drifts, stopes, and shafts, driven into the hard rock of those mountains.

Granite established itself as this was going on. The town grew and prospered with the growth of the gold mining industry, if you wanted to call it that. The town acquired a grand hotel, boarding houses, saloons, salons; and a brothel, of course.

As with most mining camps in those days, there was an abundance of whiskey, gamblers, and gunfights in the streets, but things eventually settled. Soon there was law, lawyers, churches, and a school. Granite became a better place for wives and children with a municipal water system, and warm little houses cobbled together for those wives and children to live.

Shortly after the beginnings of the second war to end all wars, the year 1942, executive order L-208 basically put an end to all gold mining in that part of the world. Miners were needed elsewhere to mine minerals of a more strategic nature. Gold was not on the list of those strategic minerals. Things like chalcocite, hematite, and galena, were deemed of higher value, and gold was about all there was to places like Granite, Bourne, and Cornucopia. The populations dwindled, then the businesses, schools, churches, brothels, and saloons were shuttered and left to weather fates dictated by the wind, the rain, the summers bleaching sun, and the winter's deep snows.

Those few who chose to stay – those to old and tired to move on again – were left to a different life than the one they used to know.

Granite had been a ghost town for decades with old Otis Ford as the mayor of a population of maybe four.

Things pretty well sat that way until Richard Nixon took the country of the gold standard in 1971. Before then the dollar was hooked to an ounce of gold, the price of gold was fixed at thirty-five dollars an ounce (Troy), and all that gold was – supposedly – stashed in a place called Fort Knox in Kentucky.

After the ounce was released from its captivity to that dollar things changed around quite a little bit as far as gold mining went. In 1972 gold bullion was thirty-eight dollars a troy ounce. In 1977 it was one hundred thirty-five dollars and seventy cents. (*A gallon of gasoline was sixty-two cents.*) In 1980 gold was actually over eight hundred dollars a troy ounce for a while. (*A loaf of bread in 1980 was fifty-one cents.*)

Gold took off on a roll, investors invested, and there got to be a horde more dollars hanging around interested in mining for that gold. The gold rush of the late seventies and early eighties was on... such as it was...in that part of the world.

The gold rush of the late nineteen seventies didn't amount to much when compared to that of the previous century. There was not a mass influx of people of all nationalities from all over the world trying to get to Granite and move the earth around. Most of that gold, the easy gold, had been taken. What was left was gold hidden underground in old load mines from a bygone era. Old load mines needing the water pumped out, re-mucked, re-timbered, and driven deeper into the very rock that part of the world sat on.

An underground miner in that part of the world had become pretty much a thing read about in the local history books showing grainy black and white photographs from the years in and around 1900. All of those that had done it before were long gone, about forty years long gone in 1977, leaving a labor void that ruffled many a mining plan. There were those that knew the ins and outs of the underground to a certain extent, but they were getting on in years and from someplace else entirely.

The miners in the late nineteen seventies and early eighties did not really seem to be much like the miners portrayed in those history books. There were not nearly as many. They were mostly young men and women of a different century that had wandered up the hill, looking for work, a paycheck, and place to set their feet for a while.

In the year 1977, the year this narrative begins, most of those buildings that remained of Granite looked like the hollowed-out stories they were. Each with a personal history... a history anchored in the really not so distant past... and if a person were to set down, and listen hard enough, the wind whistling under the eaves might just pass a little of that history on.

Carl Hentz. From and interview conducted by William C. Haight for the Federal Writers' Project (1939)

"By the way, did I tell you how the Greenhorn Mountains got their name: A greenhorn came into the small mining town looking for a mine. The boys after giving him the 'once over' decided he was looking for shade. They told him that under a large tree near the camp

would be a good place to start digging. The most pleasant part of the digging would be all the nice shade he would have from the tree."

Early Winter (1977)

*I*t was mid-November, and the beginnings of the first snow of the year 1977, when Katy Gunn turned east off that ragged road Adel called the North Fork Highway.

Center Street ran past an antiquated building made of rough-cut lumber that looked like it might have been a one-room schoolhouse left over from an earlier century. Then again almost everything Katy saw after she had made that turn looked to be left over from that period in time; buildings of log or weathered brown lumber tacked up and held together with rusty nails and capped off with a roof of hand split shakes or rusty tin.

Katy's spirit was sagging and nearly gone, along with the little money she had in her pocket when she left Reedsport over on the Oregon Coast two days before. What was left of that tank of gas and the breakfast she had at the Blue and White Café down in Baker City that morning was nearly all she had left. Life for her was nearly elemental with little extra; down to nickels and dimes, an old beat-up car, and that guitar her father had left her sitting on the seat beside her.

"I guess that would be just about right, wouldn't it? I don't belong here, but I'll be damned if I know how I'm going to get out." Katy said to that old guitar case in the seat beside her as she watched the ghostly shadows of that town drifting by. "You got any bright ideas?"

Then what Katy saw was an amber light coming from the twelve pane windows of that building on the corner of Center and Main. A warm comforting light filtering through drifting flakes of amber tinted snow, and Katy thought it just might do. She slid her car into a log that probably constituted a curb of sorts and walked towards the wooden steps that lead up to a covered porch where she saw a sign that said "Granite Store" on its shingle hanging above the door.

"Now this is comforting." Katy said to herself, as the cold began to sift through her flimsy coat and begin burrowing under her skin.

She cupped her hands on the glass of one of the Granite Store's windows and looked in, not knowing what she might find.

What she saw was two men, one old and one young, with their elbows resting on a polished oaken bar, smiling at her face in that window, the younger of those two men motioning her in with a wave of his hand.

When Katy opened that old wooden door and stepped in, she felt the warmth of a wood fire rippling over her cold body. Then she felt the smell of those two cups of invitingly hot coffee in those two crockery mugs Lance and Thor had resting next to their elbows.

It was Thor, the eldest of the two, dressed in a pair of grease speckled coveralls and a raggedy coat with frayed cuffs that spoke first:

"I'm thinking you might like a cup of this coffee... unless I miss my guess?" With an easy smile filled with yellowing teeth.

Katy: "I'm thinking you might be very correct. Smells good... and warm." As she slid over next to the stove in the corner, and watched Lance pour a cup from a blackened pewter pot that was resting on the lid of that same stove.

Lance: "Pull up a chair and sit down next to the stove here. You look cold... What brings you up here this time of day?"

"I don't know as I could honestly say. I guess it just kind of happened."

Thor: "Well now there's a story."

"I need a tank of gas."

Thor: "And you don't see any gas pumps do you?"

"No, I guess I don't."

Thor: "Little lady, you ain't going to get out of here tonight. There isn't any place you're going to buy gas, not tonight at any rate, and even if there was you wouldn't be going anywhere judging by the way that snow is coming down. There will probably be ten inches out there by morning, and that car you just drove up in isn't going anywhere, I'll guarantee you that."

There was something about being called a little lady that nettled Katy Gunn a little bit. Especially, when she was in such a predicament. Especially, when she was so close to complete exhaustion.

Lance: "You won't be able to get down the hill until the county gets its blade up here, and that probably won't be till noon tomorrow. You can spend the night on the floor next to the stove if you've got a sleeping bag. The floors a little hard but you'll stay warm."

That sounded good to Katy. Even if she could get back down the road she just came up on she doubted she'd be interested in doing it. She had too many days without a decent night's rest, and that

14

fire, on this cold and getting colder night, was awfully inviting.

Thor was looking at her in a way that Katy didn't quite understand. I guess you could say it was a thing in his eyes that instilled a little trust. A thing that said he might have been where Katy was before, and it was Ok to be there.

There was the beginning of something here that Katy had not felt since she was a child. Something that Katy could not quite put her finger on, just yet. Perhaps a feeling of something that was rough cut and warm. A feeling of having something in common with the place and those close at hand

Thor: "Why don't you stay at my place tonight. The couch is next to the stove. Comfortable and warm, and I don't think anybody is going to steal your car tonight."

Now here it was, Katy had just been asked by a total stranger to spend the night with him, and to Katy it didn't seem in the least bad idea, and not really much different than she had done before.

Thor's couch was what he said it would be. It was warm, and soft, and other than Thor's occasional snore from his little room just behind the wall where she slept it was quiet. Katy opened her eyes when the daylight began to filter through the tall pine outside. She lay on that couch and watched the fire flicker for a little bit, then fell back into a slumber once again.

She awoke to Thor's bumping around in the kitchen. When it was finished he offered a cup of rather robust coffee to Katy as she lay curled and warm on the couch. She took that cup with a nod of gratitude, and looked out the window at the sun edging its way up over the mountains to the east. It was to be a sunny cold day. The snowfall had ceased during the night, and the world looked fresh... and new... with clear blue skies punctuated here and there with light white clouds.

Katy: "I need to thank you."

Thor: "The road down isn't going to be anything but snow for a while. The county will probably have a blade up here around noon. We will need to get your car dug out, but that won't be much of a job. Only eight inches or so. Until then I guess you're going to have to deal with me... You're looking for the Cougar?"

"Adel down at the unemployment agency said they might need a hand. Adel didn't really know what the job was. It wasn't even listed yet... she'd just heard."

Thor kind of laughed." You want to work at the Cougar. That's why you're up here? I was wondering about that."

"That's the name of the place. Adel didn't know what the Cougar was, she just said they needed a hand, and there was a chance I might get on. I can cook, clean, and tend bar."

"The Cougar is a gold mine. Didn't you know that?"

"I thought it was a ski lodge, or something like that. Adel said it was near a ski resort named Anthony Lakes."

"Anthony Lakes is over in that direction about twelve miles. And what Adel said is true, if you were at Anthony Lakes. We also get plenty of snow, but this place isn't exactly what you'd call a ski resort."

"Twelve miles... I can drive that."

"I don't think so. The county only plows the road this far. If you want to go to Anthony Lakes you're going to have to go back down to Baker. Then you've got to go to Haines then on up that way. That's better than eighty miles I think."

"Just great. And I need a tank of gas."

"Bud will be along in a bit I suspect. He's the sheriff in these parts and you're now his responsibility." Thor said that with a wisp of a grin on his face.

Marshal Bud Morrow found Katy at Thor's little abode on the Cougar Mine property just as he figured. He saw her car buried in the snow in front of the Store when he stopped in for that cup of coffee he always had before he started what he called his rounds. Lance told him that her name was Katy Gunn and Thor had offered her his couch for the night. Lance also said that a stranger nearly twice as old as she offering her his couch seemed a welcome relief to her.

Bud was going to make his way up to the Cougar anyway. Terry in the lab had a radiophone that worked most of the time.

The first snow of the year did what it always did. What few phones there were in Granite were down until the phone company got around to finding where that snow had pulled that phone line down and got around to splicing it back together and nailing it back up.

17

Marshall Bud wanted to call Kevin down at the county shop and asked when he thought they would get around to plowing the North Fork Highway. Bud already knew the answer to that question. He was just fulfilling his civic duty. The main thoroughfares and the ski resort would be first to get plowed. He already knew that. It didn't matter all that much anyway, because he was pretty sure the people that lived thereabouts wouldn't be bothered much. It's just the way things were that first snow of the year.

Thor was shoveling out his woodpile when Bud pulled in through the new snow and up in front of his little house on the Cougar property.

"I hear you have a boarder." As Marshal Bud got out and closed the door on his old and battered International Scout. "I saw her car in front of the Store this morning. Lance said she went with you."

Thor got that wispy grin on his face again.

Then he called out, "The Marshal's here."

Katy stuck her head up in the window.

"Morning." Is what Marshal Bud said.

Now Katy was beginning to wonder if she was in trouble with the law again... or what appeared to be the law. Here was the sheriff, or what appeared to be the sheriff, dressed in plaid flannel and denim with a sheriff's badge pinned to a sheepskin vest standing on Thor's front steps looking at her through the window.

"The counties blade has just about got the road plowed on the way up. We can get your car dug out and get you moving back to wherever it is you need to go pretty soon."

Katy could see that smile on the Marshal's face. It eased her some.

When she unwrapped herself from the heavy blanket that Thor had left her the night before she realized she didn't have any pants on, they were hanging on a nail over by the stove in the corner, so she wrapped herself in that blanket, opened the door and stood behind the screen, barefooted and pale.

"I'm out of gas. The needle is just about on empty."

"I've got a five gallon can in the back of my Scout. That'll get you down to Baker."

"Marshal...I've only got a few dollars. I'm just about broke."

Now was the time that Kenneth C Loughton arrived on the scene, as if on cue. A clean cut and polished character in a snow-covered cartoon that Katy had now become a part of… whether she knew it, or not.

"Is Terry down in the lab yet?" That was Ken asking a question of Thor while looking at Bud. He also noticed Katy standing behind the screen door of Thor's place.

Bud: "Nope. I went ahead and used the radiophone, though. Didn't figure you'd mind. You must have been right behind the blade."

Ken: "All the way from Sumpter. Who's this?"

Thor: "This is Katy Gunn, all the way from San Francisco."

Katy got the feeling that she might have done a little more talking than she usually does with strangers in strange places in the middle of the night.

19

Ken: "Hello Katy... I see Thor has you squared away."

Katy should have been embarrassed, I suppose; being introduced to a man she didn't know, in front of a sheriff she didn't know, after spending the night in the house of a man twice her age that she barely knew, while standing in the door way, bare footed, wrapped in a wool blanket. But she wasn't embarrassed. Everything seemed to be simply understood for what it was. It was as if she landed where she did, and that was Ok.

Marshal Bud

It was my understanding that Marshal Bud was always a piece of Granite in one way or another. In his early life he would come and go as the tides of life and employment elsewhere came and went.

It was also my understanding Bud had broken his ankle working in a lumber mill in the early 1960s and couldn't go back to whatever he was doing, so he came back to Granite full time to work a few placer claims and find a little gold.

How he became the Marshal, I don't know. Maybe Granite felt it needed a sheriff, and he fit that part, so that's what he became.

I don't know if Grant County, Baker County, or both, compensated the Marshal, or even if he was compensated. If there was compensation it wasn't very substantial, and it most certainly didn't provide transportation.

The first time I ever saw the Marshal he drove up in front of the Granite Store in an old red and white International Scout – what folks back in those days called a Corn Binder. Affixed to that Scouts doors were some big decals; big golden decals of a sheriff's badge glued on each door.

Marshal Bud's situation in Granite, Oregon, was rather unique; that situation being the Sheriff of Granite, Oregon in the late nineteen seventies.

A lot of that uniqueness had to do with the fact that Granite was in Grant County, but on the very edge. Two steps to the east and Granite would have been in Baker County.

The best – and the least taxing on the equipment involved – way out of Granite to Canyon City, the Grant County seat, was south by southeast through Sumpter which was in Baker County. From the Sumpter junction it was a hard turn to the back to the west, along the Whitney Tipton cutoff to the headwaters of the Burnt River, then on down to Austin House, then Prairie City, followed by the town of John Day, and then Canyon City.

A person could attempt to go through Greenhorn, after climbing that twisty road running alongside Clear Creek, over the crest of the Blues, and down off what we called the Vinegar Creek Pass... if they were not in a hurry, but during the winter months that particular route wasn't very probable.

In the late seventies, there were not many telephones in Granite. In most places, at that time, in that part of the world, it was almost like they hadn't even been invented yet.

Marshal Bud's official method of communication was a radio that the sheriff's department in Canyon City had given him. He would radio in and say: "Granite Base, and all is well," at the beginning of each day while looking out the window of his cabin to see exactly how that day was going to be. However, that official radio needed to be plugged into that electrical receptacle tacked to the wall of the Marshal's bungalow, and of little use to him if he was out and about.

The Citizens Band Radio was the main form of communication for the citizens of Granite and the surrounding territory back then. Bud had one bolted to the dash of that old International Scout he drove. Most of the seventeen or so citizens of Granite proper had access to one, whether it was in the kitchen or hanging under the dashboard of an old Chevy Pickup Truck. Everybody pretty much knew what the neighbors were talking about, and everybody had a handle.

"Ringo, are you out there... come up."
"Affirmative, go ahead Bug Buster".
"Is the county blade getting close?"
"It's about halfway."
"Is that you Lancelot?"
"Yeah, that's a big ten-four. I saw him just a little while ago starting up the Slot."
"This is Blade Man. I'm getting there."
"Ten-four... this is Bug Buster over and out."
"Lancelot... over and out."
"Hey, Ringo... the coffees ready."
"That's a ten-four Topper, be there in about five."
"Ten-four this is Topper... over and out."

The idea with the Citizen Band Radio was to just skip the massage needing to be conveyed from C.B. to C.B. around the valley, hoping the message would eventually reach the person it was intended for. Understanding, of course, that the message that started out might be a little different after being conveyed, mouth to ear, ear to mouth through several messaging participants.

23

Katy Gunn

Katy Gunn was born in year of 1947, in the city by the bay: San Francisco. She was a happy little girl in the very beginning. She giggled and played with her friends on the school's playground and in the Brooks Avenue Park until she was twelve years old. Then her daddy died.

Her mother did the best she could with what she had, which wasn't a lot. Katy's father left his plumbing tools to her mother, and his guitar to Katy. That guitar was in the seat next to Katy when she reached Granite Oregon, in the early winter of 1977.

After her father died Katy just sort of drifted, in and out, like the morning fog on the bay.

She didn't like school anymore and she didn't like her mother's new husband, so she got a boyfriend of her own. She was pregnant when she was seventeen, and had a son that she named Christopher, after her father. (1964).

Michael was not what would be considered a very steady individual as far as fathers go. He was nineteen when he got Katy pregnant. Michael and Katy never married. Michael said he considered marriage unnecessary, and Katy left it at that, not sure she would like to be tied to Michael and his way of thinking in the first place.

Michael would get a job throwing fish down on the wharf, but it never seemed to last. What he liked most was to hang out down in the Haight and Ashbury district with his friends and do nothing in particular. He would either come home to that little second story apartment that they shared on Brooks Avenue, or he wouldn't.

Eventually he and Katy got into a brawl and Katy had to put Michael down with a half bottle of Pepper Mint Schnapps or take more of a beating herself. The police found Michael sitting in the corner with a bloody rag that Katy gave him pressed against is forehead.

Katy was on welfare and food stamps and she didn't like it, but it was all she had. She would get a job waiting tables for tourist down on the wharf but those jobs never seemed to last for her any more than they did for Michael. She would be late to often or get caught stealing tip money from under coffee cups and salad bowls.

Eventually Katy got so she liked Schnapps almost as much as Michael. More fights, more beatings, and more calls from the neighbors to the police. Eventually social services felt the need to remove Christopher from Katy and put him in a foster home. Katy had visitation and could call Christopher on certain days. It was not very just to Katy's way of thinking, but that was the way it was and Katy couldn't do anything about it. Basically, Katy was left pretty much alone, disjointed, misplaced, and misunderstood, in a world that her youth wouldn't let her understand.

Michael, drunk early one Thursday morning, stepped from between two parked cars on Oak Street and was hit and killed instantly by an early morning delivery van when Katy Gunn was twenty-five years of age. She didn't quite know how to feel about the loss of Michael. What she did know was that Michael was gone, and so was Christopher's father. She and Christopher held hands and watched as Michael's ashes were scattered on the outgoing tide from the Hyde Street Pier.

Christopher was eight years old when that happened and he liked his old man quite a lot. Probably more as a friend and a buddy than a father figure. Michael took him to the zoo quite often. They always had fun when they were together, which wasn't often, but enough. Christopher also felt that his mother had a little to do with Michael's demise. So did Katy Gunn.

It was then Katy felt completely alone. She had felt alone before, but now that aloneness was overwhelming and wouldn't let go. If it weren't for her mother she would essentially be homeless, she knew that. She also knew that if she didn't change a few things in her life, those few things weren't going to make things any better.

It was one of those things that Katy heard while sitting through the first of those Alcoholic Anonymous meetings that social services suggested she attend if she wanted to have Christopher back in her life full time.

Katy didn't consider herself an alcoholic, she just considered the fact that she was going to have to be there, in those meetings, if she wanted to have Christopher back in her life in any meaningful way. That was where Katy got stuck. She couldn't really see any way she was going to be able to get Christopher back in her life at all from that chair she occupied on Tuesdays and Thursdays.

It was a statement made by a big man with a gray beard named Simon Uric, an ex-preacher from San

Antonio, Texas, that had fallen into the jug in his late twenties, and a member of AA for nearly fifteen years, that started getting under Katy's skin.

"I had to change who I was, and where I was. I had to leave the life I had known, and find a new one." That was what Simon Uric said.

What Simon said was making sense. Katy Gunn was trapped, and she knew it, so she decided to leave the only life she ever knew. She wanted to go someplace else and start all over again for her and Christopher. Katy was twenty-seven years old.

- Katy borrowed two hundred dollars from her mother's new husband, and headed north in an old Plymouth Valiant, not knowing where, not really knowing why, just going.

She worked as a cook in a roadside café and slept in a van parked out back in Lakes Head, California that winter and a good piece of the next summer. When she felt she had enough money to move on, she did.

Eventually she found herself harvesting grapes for one of the vineyards just outside Buellton. She seemed to like that kind of work; labor that required busy hands, and not much time to think about much else.

Two years later she was just about totally tapped out when she rounded that big corner on the Powder River just outside Baker City Oregon in early November of 1977. The pittance she had for money left over from hustling tables and washing dishes over in Reedsport was all but gone.

The first thing Katy Gun saw after she got through the underpass was a square cinderblock building with a sign on the door that said "State of Oregon Employment Agency."

Katy: "Is this the Unemployment Office."

Adel; "This is the Oregon State Employment Agency, if that is what you mean."

Katy "I need a job."

Adel: "I can see that.

Katy: "Huh yea, it's been awhile I guess."

Adel: "Go on down to the Blue and White, just straight ahead there. Vera will see you get fed for a couple of bucks. If you want to get a shower and a nap you can try the Western Hotel over on the other side of town. It's clean and cheap."

Katy: "The food I can do, but I guess the shower will have to wait. I need a job more than anything else."

Adel: "Sit down over there and fill out these forms and bring them back to me. There isn't much available right now, but I can see you might be willing to take a chance on a listing we don't have yet. It's a little way from here, but it might be worth a try.

There's a crow flying
Black and ragged
Tree to tree
He's black as the highway that's leading me
Now he's diving down
To pick up on something shiny
I feel like that black crow
Flying
In a blue sky

Joni Michell (1976)

Sonny

Sonny and his people had moved nearly everything they possessed from about as far east as east could get to about just as far west.

Along with them came the kitchen, the sink, the stove, the furniture, and a dog named Easy Joe. They moved nearly the whole shebang in a rebuilt four-ton hay truck stacked high with the big stuff and one heavily loaded pickup truck to haul the bits and pieces. They sat three across the seat of each vehicle, with Little Lola and Billy Shortstack sitting in the middle with the shift levers between their legs.

Nearly everything Sonny knew he had learned from his father or someone just like him. Someone wearing boots and heavy work gloves covered with sawdust and dirt. His life had evolved around the deciduous forest of Virginia and a patch of ground that could grow potatoes and corn.

There were three brothers in that family, and when Sonny was young one acre of that ground was theirs to grow that family's garden.

Not that those brothers were particularly interested in doing so, but it was their job, and they did it, with a tiff and a squabble here and there.

Over the years more children and more dogs had brought a lot of pressure on the home place and the clan was feeling the need to expand. Some worked in the furniture factories down in Galax, but those jobs were beginning to go away with the ebbing tides of economic fortune, along with the trees from which that furniture was made.

One of Sonny's cousins, the one they called Harley, had gone to Oregon about two years before. One of Sonny's other cousins down the road had Harley's latest telephone number. However, that number didn't do much good because Harley had since gone to a place where telephones weren't.

Sonny got a letter from Harley postmarked July 10th, 1976. A letter containing a note written on the back of a bar napkin that said Elkhorn Saloon: "Hey, cousin. P.O. Box 24, Sumpter Oregon. I check it every time I get down there."

Eventually Sonny got a call from Harley. A call made on that payphone sitting outside the Elkhorn Saloon, in about the first of August of that same year. Harley told Sonny what he had heard and it did not seem a bad idea to Sonny's way of thinking at the time.

"They need someone to cut timber for the underground," was what Harley told Sonny, and Sonny had the sawmill to do the job.

Sonny's father figured it would be Sonny to go. Sonny was the oldest and the one showing the tendency to move on, but why Sonny decided to go so far west was beyond him.

"Why you want to go clear out there? What makes you think they got more out there than we got here?"

"I got the word they need timber for a mine out there in Oregon. Me and Victor could make some good money out there I'll betcha. We could make a few improvements on this old place." That's what Sonny said as he looked the home place over, with it's the rundown roofs and broken windows.

It was better than twenty-four hundred miles they needed to travel to get the lay of the land in a place called Granite Oregon, for Sonny wanted to guarantee sure footing before he moved Maggie and Billy Shortstack to a new place and a new life about which they didn't know much.

He and Victor traveled in a 1965 Buick Special that first trip.

First, it was Charleston, and then it was Lexington. Then it was Louisville, then St. Louis, then Kansas City.

They drove with their arms out the windows during the heat of the day, and those windows rolled up during the chill of the night, swapping seats when they would fatigue. At first six hours in the driver's seat, then it was four, then it was three. Taking naps in the passenger's seat, and then a meal, and a shower, to freshen up in a Truckstop along the way.

It was somewhere near Lincoln Town, out there in Nebraska that Sonny and Victor saw the sun rising over the prairies in the rearview mirror.

The prairies weren't something they were used to. They knew of them, but that was just about it. They had never seen that much flat. Sonny had always been able to see from skyline to skyline in every direction, north, east, south, and west, but it had never occurred to Sonny that the skyline could be that far away. It made him wonder what was up ahead. It made him a little lonely for the mountains back home, and they were only about halfway to where they wanted to go.

The part of Wyoming lying up against the Rocky Mountains was a rather bleak and bouldery place to Sonny's way of thinking. He began to wonder a little bit more about what lay ahead, as he leaned against the fender and looked up at that rocky landscape, while Victor tightened the lug nuts on the spare. The Rocky Mountains were also a bit of a disappointment on that end of things.

Sonny was expecting a steep rocky climb and descent, but the interstate just went up one side of the Rockies and down the other without much show.

Somewhere between Ogden and Brigham City in Utah they could see the Great Salt Lake and that great white desert expanse to the west. This was also a place that Sonny heard about, and he was wondering again, about what lay ahead.

Then it was Twin Falls and Boise in Idaho, through fields of spuds and later the orchards with peaches ripening, then across the Snake River into Oregon – fields of corn, then more sagebrush.

Then Baker City. From there it was a hard left for another forty-five minutes and a place called Sumpter.

What Sonny saw then was a forest he had never seen before. Back in Galax the forest were a mixture of mostly oak and maple with some pine here and there. A deciduous forest for the most part. A woodland that shed its leaves in a cascade of yellow, orange, and red in the fall of the year. What Sonny saw when he looked out of the window of that car as he and Victor began climbing that grade just out of Sumpter was a forest of pine and fir; a forest of

33

conifer that stayed green all year round, spring, summer, fall, and winter.

Then it was Granite. What Sonny saw then was pretty much what Harley said it was, a ghost town, with ramshackle buildings sitting at the top of a big green meadow, and for some reason Granite felt like something Sonny thought he could get comfortable with. It wasn't home, but there was something about the place; maybe a bit of familiarity that he felt he might get used to.

They found Harley all right enough. It was just a matter of luck. They pulled up beside Marshal Bud Morrow and Thor who were tinkering under the hood of the Marshal's old International Scout.

"Harley, yeah... I know Harley. He lives up in Greenhorn... up that way, but you can catch him when he gets off shift up at the Buffalo. Just head up the road. You'll see the sign. Park there. He'll be along in about forty minutes."

Hillbillies

Apparently, there was a dispossession or something of that nature in the past that left Sonny with a sour taste in his mouth as far as banks go. He knew what a checkbook was, but he didn't own one. Probably because he didn't have a bank account to hook that checkbook too. He carried money to pay for what was needed in a leather pouch in his pocket. Everything was paid for in cash. Money dealt out in round numbers: ones, fives and tens.

"If it don't get paid for it don't get got."

If it got broke it got fixed. If it needed a re-build... it got rebuilt. If it needed built the lumber was sawed on the family mill. That was Sonny and his family's life, and had always been.

"Yea, I'm a Hillbilly." Victor was comfortable with that appellation. After all, he was his father's son.

Up until the time I met Sonny and those folks that eventually showed up in Granite from the Blue Ridge Mountains in Virginia I had the stereotypical idea about what a Hillbilly actually was. (Still do, in a lot of ways.). The Hatfield's and McCoy's, Snuffy Smith, Lil' Abner and Daisy Mae, The Beverly Hillbillies; floppy hats, bare feet, and an old Easy Joe sleeping on the porch.

However, I soon got the feeling that a "Hillbilly" was also something else; something a little more tangible. I got the idea that a Hillbilly was also a person that had managed to maintain a comfortable distance from the trappings of modern civilization

35

with all its quirks and foibles. Close enough to avail oneself of the civilized niceties, but not to close. Kind of like stepping back in time a hundred years or so and still being able to buy a comfortable pair of Converse tennis shoes down at the local mercantile.

Sonny and Maggie were looking at that house, while Billy Shortstack and Easy Joe were frolicking in the trees.

Sonny and Maggie were looking at an old house with wobbly stairs running up the outside wall to the second story bedroom; an old clapboard house quite probably built a few years before the beginning second world war; that old rough timbered house with what was left of a hand split shake roof built to shed a heavy winter's snow.

Maggie: "What are we doing here."
Sonny: "I don't rightfully know as I could honestly say right now… It seemed like a good idea at the time."

What Maggie was looking at was a crooked old house sitting on a river rock foundation that needed its current tenants removed; those furry four-legged tenants who had probably occupied the place since birth.

What Sonny was looking at was free rent and an hourly wage in exchange for the saw mill that he and Victor needed to get set up and running before the snows of November arrived. *(Probably one of many non-taxable deals made along the way.)*

Then Maggie opened the rickety door to have a look inside, all the while thinking about the green grass of home.

> *The old home town looks the same*
> *As I step down from the train*
> *And there to meet me is my Mama and Papa*
> *Down the road I look and there runs Mary*
> *Hair of gold and lips like cherries*
>
> *It's good to touch the green, green grass of home*
> *Yes, they'll all come to meet me, arms reaching,*
> *smiling sweetly*
> *It's good to touch the green, green grass of home*
>
> *The old house is still standing tho' the paint is*
> *cracked and dry*
> *And there's that old oak tree that I used to play on*
> *Down the lane I walk with my sweet Mary*
> *Hair of gold and lips like cherries*
>
> *It's good to touch the green, green grass of home*
>
> *Curly Putman (1965)*

I guess the first thing Maggie decided was that house they were looking at would just have to do. Then she decided they had a plentiful amount to do and barely enough time. Winter was coming and they all knew it. They started on the morning of the twenty sixth of August, the summer 1977.

They rehung the doors and replaced broken glass. They rehinged the cupboard doors and installed new kitchen counters, cabinets, and installed the sink that they had brought with them.

37

By the second week of September the hand split cedar shingling left over from the nineteen forties had been removed and that house was reroofed with shiny new tin and the porch was painted a light spring leaf green.

That newly roofed outdoor privy would have to do. Maggie knew that. There was a brand-new toilet seat bought down at the hardware store in Baker City covering the original hole.

When all was done there was fifty pounds of flour and a sifter in the cupboard next to the twenty-pound bag of sugar: yeast, salt, Crisco, and powdered eggs. The bread was raised on Wednesday mornings and baked Wednesday afternoon, but things weren't quite the same for Maggie.

Maggie was a stout woman with a homegrown sort of disposition. In the Blue Ridge Mountains back home she cooked, sewed, canned and bartered the neighbors for eggs, onions, and gallon jugs of milk with fresh whole cream on top.

In the year 1977, in the Blue Mountains of Eastern Oregon, she didn't quite know what to do.

Maggie never drove an automobile before, then she had too. She never had a license, and she was forty-two years of age. The first time she drove Sonny's jeep down to Sumpter so the kids and the cousins could catch the school bus she never shifted out of second gear. She didn't know how to drive a clutch.

This from an interview conducted for by William C. Haight for the Federal Writer's Project in 1939. An interview conducted with a lady named Neil Nevin, a school teacher in the Granite Oregon of the eighteen eighties.

"Oh! I'm delighted! I've wanted to see the story of Granite preserved for a long time. The little town is filled with rich, boisterous lore. Rollicking, rough, and ready, would best describe those townspeople."

"Granite, or Independence, as it first was called, was built in the heart of the Blue Mountains. As you know, many creeks roar down from the mountain springs into the canyons. The mountains are rough, tower high into air and flatten out into rocky, almost impassable flats at other places. This rough country presents many obstacles hard to overcome. The rough- ness, coupled with the unfavorable climatic conditions are, at times, almost unbearable. The Granite country could be and usually is nature at its best and worst."

"Each season of the year presented peculiar problems. The fall was the best time for everyone. Then the days were warm and pleasant, fading into cool, brilliant, moonlit, starlit nights. The air brought a fresh, crisp, tang to your nostrils. The smell of the pine needles was always sharper in the fall."

Cecil

Cecile was born in Council Idaho in 1950. His mother and father never seemed to get along, so they decided to part ways, after he turned fifteen (1965). His father went south to make money rough necking oil rigs down in Texas, leaving him residing with his mother and his maternal grandparents. Grandpa was tough on Cecil. Called him a lazy hippie more times than Cecil wanted to hear, so when he turned seventeen he dropped out of school, told his mother goodbye, and headed down south to find his dad.

Cecil caught a ride from just outside Council to the Oklahoma border with a man named Jasper who talked a lot about what his life used to be. As Jasper's truck rolled down the highway he spoke about his wife and his kids and how he hardly ever got to see them. Jasper said that he was born and raised on a little farm back in Missouri, but the soil turned to dirt, and his father couldn't pay the bank what was owed. Then the farm and all that went with it sold at auction.

There was a little money left over after the debts were paid, so his father bought an old truck, and seeing as Jasper was his son, truck driving became a family tradition of sorts.

It seems Cecil was always angry at something. He never was quite sure what he was angry at, or with, or why, but he knew where he got that tendency. He got it from his daddy. There were a few times it didn't take many a beer to turn a conversation with a total stranger into a fight.

Cecil always had a problem with authority, one way or another. Understandable, I suppose, considering authority in his life was what it was. His father was around too little or too much. His mother was always somewhere else besides where Cecil was, and his Grandpa considered him a nuisance and made no bones about telling Cecil what he thought.

Cecil found his father living in a trailer park in a place called Mineral Wells down there in Texas. It didn't take very long after he found his old man that he hooked up rough necking and throwing chain on the same rig, and it didn't take all that long before he and his old man got into a fight and he lost that job.

Cecil then decided he would like to see old Mexico. He got into a fight in Juarez with a man that looked a lot like his father and got to spend a few days in a Mexican jail. The Policia took the money rolled up in his pocket and told him to go home. Cecil said he was never going to come back, as Jorge opened the door for him at the borderline and wished him a pleasant goodbye.

He managed to get a job shoveling asphalt in the New Mexico sun for a while. Then he got a job bumping knots on a log deck back home in Idaho.... for a while. Then he cooked short order up in Kalispell through the coldest part of the winter in the year 1976.

Cecil wasn't inclined to look for anything to settled. He never even thought about it much; that settled life. If what he was doing didn't work out, or he didn't like it, which was more likely, he'd look to the cash in his pocket and move on with what little he had, which was enough for him.

Cecil eventually hooked up with a job changing the oil and greasing long haul trucks in a place on the Snake River called Farewell Bend near the Oregon, Idaho border. It suited him well enough. He liked being close to the Snake River. He was driving an old pickup truck with a camper shell and a dented Grumman canoe tied on top at the time, and he would camp anywhere along the river road between Huntington and Richland that suited him. If he had a craving for hot water he would shower in the truck stop's facilities where he worked.

On his days off it was Ontario, but he began thinking of Baker City. It was farther away from Farewell Bend than Ontario, but it did have its attractions. Perhaps it was a place he'd heard of called Cattle Kate's. It would have been the sort of place to attract someone like Cecil. He also had it in mind to stop by the local unemployment agency there and see if he could find a job that required a little less greasy toil. He was hoping to find a job cooking short order, indoors, as November's winter chill began to take its bite.

"May I help you?" Adel asked as Cecil came through the door.

"Is this the Unemployment Office?" Asked Cecil, knowing full well it was, since there was the official sign stenciled on the door in the official gold lettering that all of the state's offices carried.

"This is the Oregon State Employment Agency... if that's what you're looking for," was Adel's reply.

Adel heard it referred to as the "Unemployment Office" before and had no problem correcting the error for all who cared to make it. The fact of the matter was a freckled, dusky blond, tired and worn lady named Katy Gunn had wandered in and inquired if it was the "Unemployment Office" earlier in the day.

"I'm looking for a job," Cecil said.

"Is that so?"

"I've been a driller's helper, laid asphalt, worked in the woods. I've set choker. I've worked on big oil rigs. I've done some short-order cooking."

"Well, isn't that an interesting resume. Do you have one of those? A resume?"

"No, I never needed to worry about one of those before ...What exactly is a resume?"

"Not that important right now, I suppose. Not for a person in your profession. There isn't much right now, with winter coming on, but we do have this. It just came in. There is a good chance you could get on if you can be there on Monday at about seven."

Ecuador

Timothy's O'Leary's only job in Ecuador was logging core and mapping a potential ore body for a little – first time doing anything in Ecuador – mining company named Little John.

Little John and Associates had about three core drills out in a patch of rainforest along with about six small trailer houses for Timothy and the people who were doing the drilling to reside.

There was also a shower room that ran off the same generator that powered the lights, rock saws, and crushers that resided in a roofed gazebo sort of affair that kept Timothy's, maps, logbook, and core boxes out of the nearly perpetual rain... for there was never a real end to the rainy season in that part of the world.

Before Ecuador Timothy O'Leary was a student at U.C. Berkeley in the year 1975. When he graduated he asked around among the people he got to know while studying geology and found out about place in Ecuador that needed someone to log core and do a little geology on the side. Professor Juwita referred to it as an "Entry Level" proposition. That, and the fact that the job was in Ecuador tweaked Timothy O'Leary's twenty-five- year-old curiosity more than just a little bit.

Timothy O'Leary didn't know a word of Spanish when he disembarked the plane in Guayaquil.

He was standing in the concourse of the Guayaquil Areopuerto, such as it was, wondering what his next move should be. It was then that Hermenegildo Hidrovo, who spoke a very broken English, a fair Spanish, and the local dialect of Quichua, coaxed him into a rather well used looking Piper J3 for the five hundred miles south east trip to a little town called Los Encuentros. From there Hermenegildo hauled Timothy in a battered 1962 Ford pickup truck with cattle racks, on a road of sometimes rock, sometimes mud, to the drill site about forty miles distant.

It was here Timothy O'Leary would spend nearly a year of his life, learning how to navigate jungle terrain, and learning to speak the local lingo, to a degree. Least ways enough of the local lingo to make himself fairly well understood by the local working class. Least ways as much as the local working class was going to understand someone like Timothy O'Leary.

Timothy had Merriam Webster's English to Spanish Dictionary for Students – library edition – that he picked up for fifty cents in the used book bin on his way out of the library there on the Berkeley Campus, shortly after he'd a quick look at another book titled "Ecuador."

"Dónde duermo con las cajas del núcleo?" Is what Timothy O'Leary said.

"They ees under the truck." Is what Hermenegildo said, with a bit of a laugh. His helper on the drill, Zenon, also got a bit of an indulgent smile on his face.

Timothy O'Leary just held out that dictionary and shrugged, as if to say, "Well... what do we do now?"

*H*ermenegildo was bilingual, for the most part. That made him liaison between Timothy O'Leary, Little John, and the seven people that Little John and Associates employed.

Hermenegildo was also the person in that made everything fit together, that much was obvious. He knew how to do about everything, from flying Little John's plane and getting supplies delivered, from running a drill to fixing it, to smuggling Colada de Avena onto the mine site... despite Little John's whishes on the matter. It wasn't long before Timothy began calling Hermenegildo, El Jefe.

Timothy and Hermenegildo, along with the rest of the crew became friends, even if they couldn't understand one another a lot of the time. The nights were often spent playing a card game called Cuarenta and drinking Colada de Avena under the generators light in that gazebo after a day's work.

Little John himself arrived on the prospective mine site and gave out the last of the paychecks on November 7, 1977. He also gave Timothy a piece of paper with the name Kenneth C. Loughton and a phone number on it.

"Give Ken a call when you get back. He's got a little project and he might need a geologist. Tell him you work pretty cheap."

Little John and Associates ran out of money about the time the rainy season really took hold and took big pieces of road along with it.

That left Timothy standing in a rather awkward place. That awkward place being forty miles from a little town called Los Encuentros, in Ecuador, South America, with a three hundred fifty-dollar check written on an American Bank in his hand, and the road back-home nearly washed away in front of him.

It took two days on what was left of that road in the back of a cattle truck with Hermenegildo Hidrovo and two mules to reach Los Encuentros. One of those mules was named Lucy en el Cielo, the other named Suzy del Río. Timothy had won a card game in the back of that cattle truck, and in so doing, the right to rename those two mules.

Imagínese en un bote en un río
Con árboles de mandarina y cielos de mermelada
Alguien te llama, respondes muy despacio
Una niña con ojos de caleidoscopio
Flores de celofán de color amarillo y verde.
Elevándose sobre tu cabeza
Busca a la chica con el sol en los ojos
Y ella se ha ido
Lucy en el cielo con diamantes
Lucy en el cielo con diamantes
Lucy en el cielo con diamantes

Lennon /McCartney (1967)

From Los Encuentros, Hermenegildo flew Timothy, in Little John and Associates Piper J3, back to Guayaquil, where Timothy O'Leary was able to cash that three-hundred-and-fifty-dollar check and buy a plane ticket directly to Los Angeles California for one hundred twenty-eight dollars. He then gave Hermenegildo twenty-five hundred Sucre for his trouble and thanked him for his help and his friendship. Twelve hours later he landed in Los

Angeles, California, where his mother picked him up and asked him where he'd been.

The next day he paid seventy-five dollars for a ticket and boarded a Greyhound bus headed north, looking for a place called Granite Oregon.

Timothy O'Leary Arrives

Timothy O'Leary, his back pack, his duffel bag, his suit case, along with a ragged looking manila envelope containing important documents got off the bus down there at the Antlers Hotel in Baker City, not really knowing what to do or where to go. There was one thing he was sure of, however. He needed a place to stay out of the cold; something he had to get used to because he had never really been much beyond cool in his entire life.

He had gotten off a plane in L.A. not two days earlier. His mother had picked him up in L.A. and took him back to Santa Barbara where he got on a Gray Hound Bus bound north.

He swapped buses in a place called Weed near the Oregon, California border and ended up in a place called Baker City, Oregon, on the Wednesday before Thanksgiving, 1977.

The snow was piled near knee deep at the curb where he stepped off that bus, clad in a pair of battered leather hiking boots, an old sun faded olive drab pair of pants and a vest with eight pockets in it. One of those pockets had a compass, another a pack of Delicados Cigarillos. He was also wearing a brand-new looking sock hat and a red and white checkered flannel shirt that he might have bought in Weed while he was changing buses.

What he really wanted when he finally arrived in Baker City was a warm place to sleep, and he wanted that sleep to last a long time, in a for real bed, in a place that wasn't moving.

There was a matronly looking gray haired lady with a set of spectacles on the end of her nose sitting behind an old oaken desk looking out the window of an old building made of red brick and peeling green paint that bore a sign that said "Greyhound Bus – Leave the Driving to Us."

"I need to find a room." Is what Timothy said as he walked through the door.

"Fifteen dollars for a single," was Joanna's reply.

It was here that Timothy O'Leary got a puzzled look on his face. "I don't think I've got... Wait a minute." It was here that Timothy reached into his pocket and pulled out a handful of Ecuadorian Sucre wadded up with and mixed with American Dollars.

It was here that Joanna got a smile on her face, as she looked at Timothy O'Leary over the spectacles sitting on the end of her nose. "I can see by your tan that you've been down south a ways."

Timothy O'Leary was born across from Butterfly Beach, in Santa Barbara, California, in the year 1949. He learned how not to drown in the ocean before he was eight. Surfing became a way of life for Timothy O'Leary. When he was a child the boards were made of wood, eight feet long, and too heavy for him to even pick up. When he was fourteen he would perch his board on his head, walk across Channel Drive, out across the sand and salt grass, then down that little trail to the beach below.

By 1970 Butterfly Beach had morphed into a nude beach. I don't know if the city of Santa Barbara endorsed certain beaches nude beaches, or if people really didn't need cloths for anything other than social propriety and things just turned out that way. I guess that to Timothy O'Leary's way of thinking naked people became the norm; all different sizes, shapes and colors. I also think that was the way Timothy O'Leary saw most people… no matter who they were…no matter where they were… clothed or not.

Timothy O'Leary was getting restless. Ever since he was a child he'd get the fidgets. He never could sit still for very long, and the fact that he was doing nothing more than laying on a squeaky coil spring mattress looking at the brownstone wall across the street from the Antlers Hotel on Thanksgiving Day didn't help much.

He called his mother on the pay phone sitting on the corner just down from the Eltrym Theater a little after dark. They talked until he ran out of quarters. Then he thought about seeing the movie advertised on the marquee. He had been away from theaters for nearly a year. He had heard about "Close Encounters of the Third Kind" by way of eavesdropping on a couple of Hare Krishna at the L.A. airport a few days earlier, but for some reason he just couldn't get interested.

He could feel one of those flights of fancy coming on. It didn't take very long when he had nothing on which to center his mind, so he began to walk between those berms of snow piled on the sides of the sidewalks on Main Street, looking for what Main Street had to offer.

Soon enough he came to a place called Cattle Kate's. One of the main get together places for young and old in the community of Baker City at the time.

Cattle Kate's was a bar and grill; at times a noisy place; at times rowdy place, but not always.

This night was the eve of Thanksgiving Day. Those who had finished the day's celebrations and wanted to get out of the house were there, along with those who had no place else to go. Those like Timothy O'Leary and Cecil.

Cecil was looking at what was left of the grease under is finger nails, when Timothy O'Leary walked in; looking totally out of place: tanned dark brown, blue eyes, wearing faded olive drab trousers with a lot of pockets, and a baggy flannel shirt that looked like it had been purchased the day before. On top of all that Timothy wore a new blue sock hat, with a fuzzy red knit ball on the crown, covering shoulder length sandy blond hair.

"Well, what do we have here?" Cecil was not by nature the curious kind, but something about Timothy O'Leary was tweaking his mind.

Timothy sat down at the bar, ordered a beer, flipped one of the last of his Delicados Cigarillos out, and laid the pack on the bar. Then he smelled the odor of something he suddenly realized he been dearly missing.

Cattle Kate's was also the home of fine greasy hamburgers. Hamburger's wedged between toasted sesame seed buns; slathered with mustard, catsup, and mayonnaise; served with slabs of melted cheese. Fine greasy hamburgers piled on high with fresh smelling onion, pickles, tomato, and leafy lettuce, and all that surrounded with nearly a cord of fresh whole cut fries.

Cecil: "Where've you been?"

"Ecuador..." Was Timothy's reply. Then to Carrie, behind the bar: "Excuse me Senorita... I'd like a hamburger with everything on it... and extra fries."

Carrie: "Senorita, huh... Would you like to see the menu... Senior?"

"No Senorita, that won't be necessary... I know what I want. A hamburger with everything on it... and extra fries."

Cecil: "Ecuador?"

"I was logging core for little company down there. They'd take the core off the drill rigs and give it to me. I'd do the logging and mapping, that sort of thing."

About that time Johnny Harrison threw his beer in the face of a big beefy logger named Danny O'Keefe, and the whole place went a little bit nuts. Danny threw a punch and missed. Then Johnny pulled Danny's shirt up over his head and they both landed in the middle of the dance floor. Then a passerby with too much time on his hands joined in. Then Darren the bouncer, then Carrie, and then the whole fracas just kind of rolled down the aisle and out the front door, leaving Johnny Harrison behind, sitting on the floor.

Timothy O'Leary had never witnessed such a thing. He was amazed at how quickly it got out of hand and how quickly it seemed to be over. Timothy O'Leary was also amazed at how unfazed Cecil was by the whole thing.

Cecil: "Ecuador? You mean like South America?"

Timothy's Delicados Cigarillo burned his fingers and he had to drop it in his beer. "Yea, I was logging core."

"Well, then why are you up here." As Cecil observed Timothy's brown skin. "It's cold outside you know?"

"The job down there was gone. The people that had the money didn't have it anymore, and Little John, my old boss, said that he knew of a guy that was opening up a mine up here that needed a geologist… if I hurried…And yeah… it is cold out there." As Timothy O'Leary looked out the window of Cattle Kate's and the snowy dark night beyond with a bit of trepidation.

Cecil: "A geologist?"

Timothy O'Leary: "A pebble pincher."

Cecil: "Where you going to be working?"

Timothy O'Leary: "It's off over there somewhere. On the other side of that rocky granite escarpment to the west."

Cecil: "The Elkhorn?"

Timothy O'Leary: "Somewhere on the other side of the Columbia Load. A town called Granite."

Cecil: "A mine called the Cougar?"

Timothy O'Leary: "That's the place."

Cecil: "Adel down at the Unemployment Office said I should be there Monday. I'm going to meet the guy that does the hiring. We might be working in the same place."

It was then that Timothy O'Leary turned and looked Cecil square in the eye, an impish little grin on his lower lip. Cecil was about to become acquainted with Timothy O'Leary's sense of humor.

"Reality is greater than the sum of its parts... also a damn sight holier."

Cecil: "What did you say?"

Timothy O'Leary: "Ken Kesey said that. I didn't."

Carrie then slid Timothy's hamburger in front of him. Carrie had a skinned-up elbow and a slight bruise over her left eye. "Do you want some ketchup for those fries... Senior?

"Por favor."

Jim and Alice

Jim was born in a red brick apartment building with the Willamette River on one side and the Union Pacific Railroad tracks on the other.

Jim's dad left he and his mother for another world when Jim was quite young. Jim's dad had been in the Laborer's Union for better than two years. He was getting to a place where the work was a little steadier and the pay a little better when a Manitowoc Crane let a load of steel beam down and he could not get out of the way (1962). Jim's dad was twenty-five years old.

He left Jim and his mom not much more than a box of rusty tools and a savings account with five hundred dollars. Jim and Mona got by, but that was just about it. After the rent was paid there wasn't much left, so Jim had to learn how to innovate and invent.

Jim cobbled a motorcycle together out of the neighborhood's leftovers with his daddy's box of tools when he was fourteen years old.

Jim did not have much luck staying out of trouble with civil authority back in those days.

His troubles probably began when he was building a big firecracker out of a cardboard paper towel tube when he was fifteen. (1973)

He found a book that told how the ancient Chinese made black powder down at the local library. He bought potassium nitrate down at the pharmacy. All he had to do was go to the counter and asked for it. He bought sulfur down at the nursery, and then he took some charcoal briquettes and hammered them down to a fine powder with a hammer from his father's tool chest for the carbon. Fuse was the problem. It just could not be purchased down at the hardware store, so Jim tried to make fuse out of rolled toilet paper and some of the black powder he had manufactured. That homemade fuse burned a little fast and Jim did not get out of the way before things went a little awry. That firecracker burned with a loud flash and caught the dry brush on fire between the Union Pacific's railroad tracks and the Willamette River, and Jim couldn't get it put out with his flailing shirt before the law enforcement showed up.

After that the police kept a closer eye on Jim. His next infraction was driving a motorcycle underage and without a license.

Alice was his neighbor down the street back then. He would walk by on his way to school and she would be standing on the steps to her mother's place. He and she would share that walk together, and as time passed they became an item, seen together almost every day.

When Jim was seventeen he cobbled an old Studebaker station wagon back into running condition, and when he turned eighteen he graduated from High School, much to his mother's surprise.

Work in that part of the world was not for eighteen-year-old boys, however. He had to stand in line behind all those ahead of him down at the Union Hall waiting his turn, and the line was long.

Jim's options weren't many, so he got into more trouble with the law when he was stealing a tire off an old car that was not worth much. He was loading the tire in the back of his Studebaker when a cop pulled up and took him into custody. He did two days in jail before his mother got him out on his own recognizance that time. Next, he stole the car.

When Jim was twenty he could see he wasn't going to go much of anywhere where he was, so he decided he'd just go someplace else.

He had heard about the latest gold rush in Eastern Oregon on his mother's old television, so he thought he'd give gold mining a try. He didn't know exactly where he was going to go; he was just going to go. He knew he wanted to change something, but he didn't even really know what that something was.

Alice was sitting on the steps of that old apartment building watching Jim load his possibilities into that old Studebaker.

"Going east?"

"Yup"

"Leaving pretty soon?"

"Yup...." Then he gave Alice that smile that she liked to see. "Want to go?"

Alice's life was a lot like Jim's. She was out of school, sitting on the porch, not going much of anywhere, so just as well pick it up and move it on.

"Let me get my suitcase and some sandwiches." She was already packed.

The mother's probably worried when they got the notes that said their children were living in sin and gone to find gold. The idea probably seemed thoroughly preposterous. But then again, it was something, even if no one seemed to know what that something was.

All his life Jim listened to the noise of machinery. He didn't know he was hearing it, but he was. It was either the rumble of a train, the thrum of a barge, a horn on the river, or the sound of heavy trucks moving steel down at the end of the street. It was always there. It never went away.

Jim: "Listen."

Alice: "I don't hear anything but the creek and a bunch of birds."

"That's what I mean... Listen."

This from a man named Carl Hentze, a miner in that part of the world in the eighteen eighties. Mr. Hentze was interviewed by William C. Haight for the Federal Writers Project in 1939.

"Fizzle Number 13 is a regular woman. I have never seen anything like her. She beguiles me, taunts me. Damn her, she will lead me on with little pockets of $10 or $20, then abruptly stop. Fizzle holds something and by Jiminy Jack I am going to get it"

Thor

Thor was missing a piece of the index finger above the third knuckle on his right hand, and piece of the thumb above the second knuckle on his left. He lost that piece of his index finger between the bull and worm gears on a heavy winch in 1936. He lost that piece of his thumb because he got carless with a table saw.

He also walked with a slight limp from the time a log rolled off the log deck and pinned him up against a rubber-tired skidder, breaking his leg in two places, once above the knee and once below. Close enough to the joint to make the healing difficult and a little incomplete. That was one of the many near misses and direct hits that were again manifesting themselves as a few the aches and pains of old age in the winter of 1977.

Thor was born in the year 1915 somewhere over near the mouth of the Umpqua River in Coastal Oregon. He was the son of a fisherman in the very beginning, and that probably would have been his life also, if dry land didn't offer a stronger beckoning.

He started dragging cable and setting choker on trees nearly as big around as he was tall for a highline outfit when he was eighteen years of age. (1933). He learned how to run the Donkey and then he learned how to fix it. Then he learned how to splice heavy cable. Eventually he learned how to rebuild heavy gears with an arch welder and grinder from those that already knew how and were willing to show him. He eventually learned how to repair or rebuild just about everything made of steel, iron and brass in those woods.

Thor met a woman named Doreen Lindstrom and married her when he was twenty-one years old (1937). Then Thor and Doreen had a baby girl named Sally. (1941)

World War II started about a week after Sally was born and Thor was conscripted into the army in December of 1942. Many mechanics were required during WWII and Thor was put to work keeping tanks and trucks running in Tallahassee Florida and then in England and then in Northern Europe. When he finally got home to stay Sally was better than four years old and barely knew who he was. Something that Thor set about rectifying as soon as he could. It was probably that time apart that made Doreen and Sally more precious than ever to Thor.

There was something about Sally that Thor loved more than anything else. He couldn't quite put his finger on what that something was, but it was definitely there. Maybe it was the way she looked at the Steller's Jay that robbed her of her cracker; that look of easy amusement. Maybe it was that easy appreciation of nearly everything as if it were new, shiny, bright, and special. Whatever that something was often caused him to linger over his morning coffee longer than he should when Sally would get out of her warm bed in the dark of the early, early morning to say goodbye.

When Sally was thirteen (1954) and Thor was thirty-nine he thought it might be kind of nice to get out of bed in the morning and not get rained on every day during Oregon's long wet coastal winters. Thor said he had heard of a place that wasn't quite so wet on the other side of the state. Doreen agreed. At that time, she felt it would be a good change.

The summers were satisfactory in Sumpter, but the winters traded rain falling from the sky for the constant knee deep of the winter's snow.

Thor and Sally thrived in Sumpter, but Doreen just never seemed to catch on. Not that Doreen was opposed to the rural way of life, but Sumpter was just a little more rural than she had originally anticipated.

Doreen's mother died in January of 1956, and her father, who was getting on in years, moved in with her brother in Florence. That was where her family was from and that is where she wanted to be, so Thor and Doreen decided that a move back to the coast would not be all that bad of an idea. Thor was going to stay in Sumpter until Doreen and Sally were moved and situated, and then he was going to follow as time and work allowed.

It was in the early spring of 1957 that Doreen and Sally were headed back to Florence to see Doreen's father and look for a place to settle and live. They had just crested Dooley Mountain Summit and started the downhill glide when the Buick they were in went over the side for reasons unknown. That car eventually stopped rolling and landed on its wheels in the valley below, taking the life of Thor's wife and daughter.

Doreen and Sally were buried somewhere near the mouth of the Umpqua River because it was the place Doreen knew best. Those in Sumpter that knew Thor knew that he had Doreen and Sally.

Then they knew he was all alone. Then, one day, they noticed that he was gone.

Apparently, Thor spent his time moving up and down the coast trying to get his bearings, but without much success. He eventually made his way back to Sumpter because he couldn't figure any place else to be.

He finally settled into a life of keeping the machinery running for folks that couldn't afford to get it fixed right away; folks that said they could give him ten dollars down, which they often didn't have, and were willing to pay the rest when they could, which they often couldn't. It kept his mind and his hands busy until the numbness that permeated his life since Doreen and Sally had gone away began to wear off a little.

Eventually Thor settled into a life that was part of Granite. If it got busted and needed to be fixed, whether it was a snow mobile, the gear box on a 1965 Ford half ton pickup, or a D-7 Cat, and you lived west of the Elkhorn Ridge, in the Blue Mountains of Eastern Oregon, Thor was the man you sought to get it fixed.

Thor was sixty-two years of age in 1977. He was the chief mechanic for the Cougar Mine, and just about everybody else around those parts as far as that goes. He lived in a comfortable little house situated back among the pine and fir on the Cougar Mine's property, which suited him well enough.

Smokey & Angelina

I don't know what Smokey's real name was. Maybe he was born Smokey.

It's not all that hard to explain Smokey. I guess he was just what he was. He had become what was known as a tramp miner, a thing of mystery and reverence to those of us naïve and new to the profession. He had been underground busting rock nearly his whole life. He had driven Drift in Colorado, Utah, Montana, Oregon, Nevada.

I guess you could say Smokey was good at staying ahead of things. Before the job he was on finished he knew where the next was going to be. That is just the way things were: finish it up; be packed and be ready to move on.

Another way of collecting an understanding of Smokey was Angelina. They had been born in the same place in the same year, 1916. Their houses didn't quite touch, but their back yards did. Angelina once told me Smokey's dad started laughing in the middle of the night and couldn't stop when he caught her and Smokey making faces at each other through their bedroom windows.

There was the neighborhood bully that wanted to beat Smokey up when he and Angelina were both twelve years old. They were on their way to school through a grove of newly planted orange trees when that bully stepped out from that grove and stated his intention was to kick Smokey's ass. Angelina was on his back almost instantly, and that bully had to think about two things instead of one. That is the way things were with Smokey and Angelina. I guess you could say they came arranged in a package; a package of two.

Smokey wandered off when he turned nineteen. Orange picking for the season was done, so he thought he would see what the rest of the world had to offer.

It was the height of the great depression when he apprenticed himself out to the WPA driving a tunnel for the railroad up in Nevada that year, 1936. He was twenty-one when that job finished. He had a little cash in his pocket, so he came back and asked Angelina to leave the security of her home and go with him, and she did.

I do not know if they ever married, but if you knew them, and the way they were geared and fitted together, that formality would seem a little superfluous.

Eventually Angelina decided she didn't like the life they were leading. They would settle in the woods north of Rand Colorado, then they would move to a shack down on the Snake River while Smokey was driving a diversion tunnel for a dam. She was tired of that life and declared she would travel no more. She settled them in a little town near Denver, but by then Smokey was what he was and there wasn't much going to change that. He still followed the work wherever it went. There were times they would not see each other for weeks.

Eventually Angelina tired of that also. It was then she and Smokey gave up whatever semblance of a settled life they had and followed the gold boom of the late 1970s and early 80s to Granite Oregon to see what it had to offer.

Angelina said it suited her just fine. She said she was interested in a little peace and quiet and having Smokey home every night more than anything else.

You could hear Smokey and Angelina having some rather vociferous arguments at times. Those of us that lived in that big two-story house across the way – the place that most folks in that part of the world called Dog Patch – got to hear them at one time or another.

Their arguments usually revolved around something like, "The fires almost out."

"I'll get to it in a minute. Can't you see I'm busy?" Smokey was just sitting on the porch wrapped in a heavy coat.

"The fires almost out.

"Yea, yea, yea, I'll get it."

"I don't see why you don't get it now, before it goes out completely."

"Yea, yea, yea. Settle down woman. I'll get it soon enough.

"Why don't you get it now? And who you calling woman?" It seemed like Angelina was taking on a few of Katy Gunn's personality traits, just to irritate Smokey at times.

"Yea, Yea, Yea."

I guess that Smokey and Angelina's brand of argument wasn't really and argument, but an affirmation of an independence that didn't actually exist between them.

They'd known each other nearly all their lives, and they had been together nearly all their lives, except when circumstances forced them apart, and they'd fought that apartness with all their hearts... and then, in the year 1976, they'd found their up to Granite Oregon.

This from an interview with a gentleman named Carl Hentz, a miner in Eastern Oregon about 1885 or so. An interview conducted by William C. Haight for the Federal Writers Project. (1939)

"My home is on part of the location grounds of Fizzle No. 13, a mine located near the foot of Little Canyon Mountain in Eastern Oregon. The house is about a mile from a group of shacks that hover around a larger house on the side of Canyon Mountain."

"The group of miners on Little Canyon call this cluster of shacks, Gukorville. The name comes from the fellow that lives in the largest house, Ike Gukor. Ike is Mayor of Gukorville, and Dean of the Mountain. He is as much a part of the diggings in that part as the ore we muck out."

"In the evenings we grubbers, pocket hunters, hardrockers, and placer miners' hunch around the stove in Ike's house and do the best part of our mining. Say, we have panned out more millions in gold than there is in the whole durn mountain, while sitting around that stove."

"The usual group around that stove includes Ike the mayor; the old man of the mountain, another fellow there that looks like one of them Snow White dwarfs — only dirtier; Pete, a half-breed Injun; and a couple of other fellows and myself."

The Gold Dust Twins

The Gold Dust Twins weren't actually twins; not even kin. They were just a couple of guys who rode the tail end of the gold boom in Eastern Oregon, never made any money that anyone was aware of, and stayed busy at it for years.

When Richard Nixon took the country off the gold standard in 1971, I don't think he reckoned on the way such an act would affect the little burgs and towns in Eastern Oregon. Especially those little, almost gone ghost towns, like Granite and Cornucopia.

In 1971 the price of gold was fixed at $35.00 an ounce. In 1980 the spot price of gold was around $595.00, and an interestingly diverse group of people headed to those mountains, filed mining claims, and the gold rush of the late 1970s and the early 1980s was on.

Gold mining in Eastern Oregon took on as many facets as a cheap diamond. Little placer claims were resurrected, abandoned adits opened, and money was obtained from all over the country to extract the wealth from the rock and put that wealth in the pockets of the investors.

It took a little longer than a rational person would expect for the "Boom" to fizzle. It kept itself alive more on velocity than gold. I don't think Grant County realized a single tax dollar, but the bars and taverns, places like Cattle Kate's and the Granite Store, realized tidy profits, I'm quite sure.

A logging road would be cut exposing an outcrop of "likely rock" with high "mineral potential" and then a group of knowledgeable speculators would descend on this "new find" to begin making deals, exchanging contracts and various other agreements to extract the gold bearing "material" from the ground.

Although no one ever got close to getting rich off any of the enterprises in Eastern Oregon at the time, the market price of all mineral "prospects" stayed high: $1,000,000.00; a nice round number and easy to remember.

There was always just enough gold to maintain an interest, and more to be found "down just a little deeper", according to "assay results", but "Getting Rich" was a lot more difficult than anticipated and a lot harder work than most were inclined to do.

Gold would turn to copper, platinum would turn to sliver, and rich veins guaranteed to yield gold kings never really seemed to materialize. Soon an investor's money would be gone.

The people who agreed to do the work on "speck" were accused of stealing what little gold there was, and those who owned written contracts often got just that... the paper that those contracts were written on.

Impinged contracts hammered out on old Underwood typewriters and bar napkins made their way down to the county courthouse. Cases were argued with much personal insult by speculators who couldn't afford attorneys, and mining companies that didn't have any visible business structure. People were sued, counter sued, and resued, and vast mineral enterprises were literally destroyed in small claims court.

Later than sooner the realization began to seep in the collective personality that perhaps this gold thing really wasn't what it was cracked up to be. The Quicksilver Mining Company became the Quicksilver Construction Company, and Harding's Mining Supply became a Harding's Hardware Store.

This is the area where Myron and Woody, who became known as the "Gold Dust Twins" – by a derisive peer group – found their niche; in the swirl of paper vortexed up behind Eastern Oregon's rapidly downward spiraling gold rush.

I had also found my niche. A place of employment where the paychecks would cash every so often – a requirement dictated by my new wife and soon to be new son – and being an "Assay Tech" for a "reputable" company, I became a person of importance in the Eastern Oregon of the early 1980s; and as such, a person of importance to the Gold Dust Twins, who would require me to do some assay work on "speck" every so often.

Myron and Woody would bring me a rock and asked for analysis to make sure they weren't being shilocked on their latest mining venture, and that the cost of analysis (a piece of what was to be my wage) be put on their account, which never seemed to be brought up to date. My boss would always allow such goings on, probably in the hope of acquiring enough leverage with the Gold Dust Twins to vest himself of an interest in a venture should one ever prove to be profitable.

I don't know why those two continued to bring me their samples because my work was always in

70

error. I would write "trace" and Myron would protest the result stating that the gold must have been "volatized"; meaning: gone up the chimney with the vapors emitting from the crucible while it was in the assay furnace.

Myron and Woody would then go to Charles, another assay person, who could always be counted on to produce the desired results.

Charles was a dowser. A dowser is a person who can, with benefit of copper rods and swinging blocks of wood, tell how much gold is available for the taking and how deep it was in the ground.

Myron and Woody would take the sample and my muffed assay result to Charles. He would place the sample in the assay furnace and take a dowsing rod with his wedding ring pressed up against the haft, and wait for the temperature of volitization to be reached. His dowsing rod would jerk wildly in the direction of the assay furnace exhaust, and Charles would declare, "There she goes", thus proving the fallacy of my assay result, the validity of the "claim", and the need to move forward and "capitalize" the project.

Myron and Woody eventually came to a disagreement needing arbitration in the judicial system. It seems some gold came up missing. Probably some paper ounces based on Chuck's assay. Myron contended Woody took the gold home in a barrel and Woody contended slander. Myron took Woody to court for the pilfered ounces and Woody took Myron to court for slandering his good name.

71

The outcome of the trial, which was settled very quickly, the verdict of which was handed down by one Judge Jackson, was that Myron couldn't prove Woody had taken ounces of gold that were no more that speculation on paper and Woody couldn't contend slander and defamation of character for the opposite reason. Woody couldn't prove he hadn't pilfered the ounces.

Woody's good name had been impinged and he would receive redress for this grievance from some quarter. He took the only avenue left open to him. He sued Judge Jackson, stating that the good judge did not like him and had failed to make an impartial decision accordingly.

I believe this to be true.

Judge Jackson did not like Woody, or Myron nor Charles for that matter. Judge Jackson regarded these people and all the people associated with them, (myself included, I suppose) to be a group of complete and total nuisances who would clutter up his docket with high theater and petty grievances.

Woody never received recompense or compensation for the insult perpetrated upon his character. However, I think he did punch Myron in the nose behind the Elkhorn Tavern up there in Sumpter and redressed the matter in that fashion.

Myron moved on after a bit; moved into a life other than that of a precious metal's entrepreneur. I believe Myron went back into the Amway business.

This is a true story. (For the most part.) I've read it over for fiction, but I can find none. (Well… maybe a little, but not all that much) These people are/were real (I changed their names) and I guess I got to be a part of this little bit of preposterous history. I would like to think I was a reasonable, non-delusional mind in the middle of this absurdity... but you never know: Gold is gold.

Mine Safety

I was sitting in Cattle Kate's Bar and Grill down there in Baker City drinking a beer and wondering what my next move in life was going to be. My job helping build log houses had gone away on the tides of latest economic recession, and I didn't have many prospects.

That was when Terry sauntered in, had a good look at my glum disposition, and had a seat at the bar beside me.

Terry and I had gone to high school together, we were friends, and we began to talk. When I told him that I had been helping build houses out of logs Terry's ears perked up a little bit. He said that he was working at the Cougar Mine up in Granite, and since there was no such thing as an underground miner anymore, he thought my log home building attributes might be refocused on timbering and rehabilitating the old underground workings. He asked if I wanted to become an underground miner… and three days later, I was one.

A very official government agency required a certain amount of instruction for a new miner, and Terry was the instructor for the five of us: Timothy O'Leary, Jim, Victor, Cecil, Katy Gunn, and I. Terry was the individual who was supposed to teach us how to do our jobs without causing calamity or coming to harm.

The tools Terry had at his disposal for that job, other than the M.S.H.A. *(Mine Safety and Health Administration)* instruction manual, was Peel's

Mining Engineers Handbook *(Circa 1918)*, a blackboard, a piece of chalk, four hard wooden benches, five stiff hot cups coffee, and his personal six months mining experience.

"This is called Spiling," said Terry, taking a piece of chalk and drawing a crude diagram of heavy steel rods driven into a clay dike over a square set. "We drive Spiling to keep the back from coming down on your head while you're standing in the next set of timber."

Then the little ding-ding of an egg timer and Terry walked through the door into the Lab next to the Training Room to check on and pour a fire assay or two. Then he stuck his head back through the doorway. "This is going to take a minute. Go ahead and take a break."

Part of M.S.H.A's required training was so many hours of first aid education.

"What are you going to do if someone gets damaged on the job," was the question Terry had to ask. "What do you do if a person gets slabbed, shatters a leg, and goes into shock?"

Timothy O'Leary, opening the nearly new, and only copy of the American Red Cross First Aid Manual to the appropriate page: "Lay the person down on a backboard, elevate that person's feet about twelve inches, unless head, neck, or back is injured or you suspect broken hip or leg bones. Begin C.P.R., if necessary. If the person is not breathing or breathing seems dangerously weak..."

Terry: "Yeah, yeah. His leg is all busted up. Get with it, Timothy. And what if you don't have a backboard handy?"

Jim: "I guess you'd have to prop him up with some rocks."

Terry acquired one of those soft rubber mannequins that a person blew air into to simulate Cardiopulmonary Resuscitation (CPR) from the fire department down there in Baker City; a life-sized, puff up, effigy of a man that looked like some sort of lobotomized rubber doll.

Terry: "Mouth to mouth resuscitation. Who wants to go first? Tilt his head back till his throat opens, pinch his nose and blow in his mouth like it shows you in the Red Cross First Aid Manual."

Katy Gunn: "I don't think that is going to happen."

Cecil: "Ah, come on Katy, give it a whirl. I'll go next."

Forty hours of instruction, coffee, hard wooden benches, and a break to flex butt muscle and stretch the back every so often, before Terry had covered all necessary and ran out of things to talk about.

Forty hours of Terry's personal instruction is what we needed before we got our M.S.H.A. certification. That billfold size paper card residing in the lunch bucket sitting on the workbench in the Dry where it wouldn't soak up moisture from the constant drip, drip, drip that permeated the air down below. That little paper card that said we were qualified to be doing what we were supposed to be doing. The certification that stated we were qualified to go underground and work.

"On the job training." Was what Terry called the next phase of our apprenticeship.

Here we were: Timothy O'Leary, Jim, Victor, Cecil, Katy Gunn, and I. We had come from assorted places to this place. We had gone from not knowing one another to knowing one another, and now we were supposedly underground miners: brand spanking new, never been there before, standing in front of the portal, wondering what to do next.

It was Smokey's job to show us the ways and whys of the underground. He was looking us over as we stood in front of him, assessing the situation as best he could; trying to decide on a good place to begin.

"This is a shovel." Was the first thing I ever heard Smokey say.

The First Day

I remember that very first day like it was yesterday. I remember walking up to a dark wet hole in the side of mountain they called a Portal. I can very distinctly remember the smell of wet cold earth blowing in my face and, "If these guys can go down there… Well, I guess I'm gonna."

I remember those timber sets in the Decline as I began my walk down. It was like seeing the rib bones of a giant snake from the inside, twisting down and close together. I remember a lot about the going down: the narrow beams of miner's lights bouncing off the rib, the back, and the floor. I remember the smell of diesel exhaust and the acidic smell of the smoke leftover from the last blast.

I remember that black mud on the floor under my feet. I remember that water dripping down from the Back– always dripping down – puddling on the floor and running down the piss ditch to number one sump.

> *Going down… underground*
> *Down into the bowls of the earth*
> *Down into the darkness*
> *There ain't no light*
> *Rock and timber all around*
> *Going down…underground.*

"Here… get this powder primed up and ready. Use that powder punch… poke a hole in the end of those sticks of dynamite and insert the caps: two naughts for the burn, six ones, six twos, four threes, and eight fours for the back and the lifters. This ground don't take much to move it, so we'll tap her nice and light."

"When I was in school they told us not to play with these things."

"Well, I guess you ain't in school anymore... are you. Tamp the powder in and wire the caps like I showed you."

"You mean stick this wooden pole down in those holes we just drilled and bang on the back of those sticks of dynamite."

"Well I guess you're just a humorous person, aren't you? Why don't you go down and find a place down at Dog Patch? I think you and me's going to get along just fine... Now tamp the powder and wire in the round."

Smokey showed me the detonator and how to wire it in. Then he let me push the go button... but he neglected to tell me to step back behind a timber set. Five loud booms from five timed explosions, and then five hefty puffs of air that ruffled my diggers and just about took the hard hat and light off my head, reinforcing the fact that I was in a different world than the world I knew the day before.

Smokey just smiled. "Now let's go eat a little lunch while the smoke clears."

Katy Gunn: "Boy! did you see all that!" (*I don't see how I could have avoided it.*) "I just mucked a round and I haven't driven anything but a Dodge Valiant before today. I'd never even heard of a mucker before I came up here. He showed me the levers, the brake, and the throttle... and I was a mucker operator. I mucked and hauled. Did you see all that down there!"

"Yea, I saw it Katy. What say we go up to that Store and have us a beer? I think I'm going to need to think this whole deal over a little bit more... what you say?"

"What?... Did you see that!... I almost got it down. I can almost run down the drift in third gear and go around that first tight turn without banging the Rib. Did you see that? I'm going to be good at this.... Beer?....Yea!"

It was when Smokey was showing me the peddles and levers and what they were supposed to do on that mucker that I noticed the steering wheel was bent off a little to the side. It was Smokey that told me about how Gabriel had gotten to far forward with the bucket on that mucker while trying to knock a big chunk of rock out of the back; a Doney nearly the size of that mucker bucket itself. That Doney slid down the boom on that mucker, and into Gabriel's lap, killing him instantly.

Terry never mentioned it during our training sessions, down there in the training room, next to the lab. Not during the forty hours of training when we were supposed to absorb what we needed to know on our way to becoming underground miners, when a person might figure on hearing about such a thing. I guess it was not exactly the type of thing Terry liked to dwell on.

It was Terry who felt for the pulse and pronounced Gabriel dead. It was Terry who had to find Alejandra's phone number – with a feeling deep down in his stomach that he said he'd never forget – and it was Terry that had to call Alejandra and tell her how Gabriel had died. It was also Terry that had to endure M.S.H.A.'s hours of investigative inquiries as to just what had happened, when, in actuality, he was not there and really did not know.

Terry spent most of his time in the Lab, the newest building on the Cougar Mine property at the time. A building made of fresh cut lumber from the mill Sonny put together on the flat up above the Portal.

Terry did not spend nearly all his time in the Lab because he was all that busy. The Lab was just a comfortable place to be. It had a two-way radio, a mobile telephone, a C.B., and warm running water, something Terry did not have in the little trailer house in which he took his meals and slept in near the whine of Sonny's mill. He hauled water to that trailer in a five-gallon Jerrycan that he specified for the job.

This from an interview conducted by William C. Haight with a gentleman named Carl Hentz who lived in Canyon City Oregon for the Federal Writers Project (1939)

"About that time one of my sisters had came to America and she wanted me to come and live with her. Once I started to go, but I received a letter from her telling me that America was suffering from a severe depression and I had better stay in Germany."

"This depression was during Cleveland's administration". (1895)

Life at the Cougar

"You know, if you don't think about smashing your thumb with that single jack, your chances might be a little better that you won't."

That was Smokey giving Jim a lesson on how to drive spikes. Jim was squeezing his left thumb with his right hand as tight as he could, as if he loosened his grip and took a good look he was going to see something he didn't want to see and it was going to hurt a whole lot worse.

Most times Smokey didn't say much at work about anything but work. Business was business for him in kind of roundabout manner.

Life at the Cougar was relatively mechanized for us at the time. There was the mucker and the drill, the things we put our hands on. Then there were the things that we didn't put our hands on. That big fan that fed the air we breathed from outside down the airbag to the Face; the fan that cleared the sooty exhaust from that diesel-powered mucker and the acidic smoke from the last blast. Then there was the compressor that compressed the air that powered the drill, and that diesel generator that powered the pumps and Sonny's mill when the unpredictable power supplied by California Pacific Utilities went away.

Mining at the Cougar was referred to as semi-skilled labor in the official registry that kept track of such things, and I guess that is exactly what it was. It didn't take much to catch on: drill the round, load the round, and touch it off. While the smoke from the blast was clearing, you ate your lunch. Then it was time to muck the round back to the muck bay and get a timber set down in the hole and stood in place.

The very first timber sets at the Cougar looked like just what they were; trees that had been felled, the limbs lopped off, cut to length, then humped down and stood in place. You could see that when you started down the Decline. The timber becomes a little more sophisticated the further down you go.

Eventually, the timber gets squared, but the lagging is no more than the slabs of wood leftover from the squaring of that timber; rough, non-dimensional, and covered with bark. At the Face all the mines timber was new and polished, all cut to dimension on Sonny's mill.

"The length of lagging usually equals the distance between the sets... Lagging on the back is usually placed skin to skin; on the sides open lagging is usually sufficient. Space between the lagging and the walls is best packed with rock. Sprags (stretchers)... are the distance pieces cut to fit between sets at the joint between cap and post and spiked in place."

Peels Mining Engineers Handbook (Circa 1918)

During the course of a typical shift in the Decline the Face was opened to a hole about nine feet wide, nine feet high and maybe four feet deep, with about twenty sticks of dynamite loaded in the holes we'd drill. After the blast, and the smoke from that blast had cleared, the round was mucked, and the timber set stood in place. The cap and the legs of those timber sets were eight inches square by about eight feet long, each weighing in at better than a hundred pounds. The legs were stood in place and the cap set on top. Then the Sprags, between the new timber set and the last set stood were set in place and spiked in place with eight-inch spikes and a heavy three-pound hammer. Then the lagging was placed between those timber sets forming a wall and a roof. On top of that roof the cribbing was stacked and wedged in tight to prevent that ground from moving.

Often a day at the Cougar was like going to the gym and working out with hundred-pound weights for about eight hours.

Then there was that shovel; always handy; always close by.

A lot of the ground at the Cougar was what Smokey called "Ravely". At times the ground was a cross between mud and fist-sized rock. After the blast a timber set had to go in as quickly as possible because that ground was going to start moving and try to fill the hole we had made.

Every so often there would be a Clay Dike that we needed to find our way through. A wall of clay is what that dike was, the quality of which could easily have been used to make pots, vases, coffee cups, and Gumby Dolls. That clay was dry when we opened that ground, but that opening would relieve the pressure, and those minuscule little pours between those fine particles of clay would want to expand and breath, permitting the water that was always dripping out of the Back start finding its way into that Dike. Water would mix with clay, and then more water would mix with more clay, in an ever-expanding perimeter. A wall had to be built, and it had to be strong, because things were going to start "moving" towards the area of least resistance, and that "moving" was not going to be easily deterred. The timbers had to be tight, and close together (back to back) and even at that, those wet clays the consistency of putty, would begin squeezing through the cracks between the pieces of Lagging that made up that wall.

Nevertheless, work isn't all work, and everybody knows this.

When Smokey found out that Katy Gunn had her daddy's guitar in the back of her old Plymouth talk of work went by the wayside and talk about folk music, guitars, and fiddles took center stage. It would seem Jim and I were shuffled off to the side of things, and Katy Gunn got extra attention in matters of guitar cording and mucker operation. She also got the best room down at Dog Patch.

Katy Gunn was the mucker operator, which was in the natural order of things, I suppose. After all, she was female and females most generally lack the physical strength to hump timber and wrestle a drill. But a person had to be careful about what was said in that regard. Although that was the real world physical reason she ran the mucker most of the time it was considered bad manners to mention the fact that she was running the mucker because she was a woman. Katy ran the mucker because she was a miner and the only person to deviate from that fact when it came time to talk about such things was

Victor, and he only made that mistake a couple of times.

Katy was a woman and she knew that. She also knew she was working in a place that belonged to a culture based on physical strength because that was just the way things were. What Katy didn't like was being treated as if she were feminine.

However, if she even considered that fact when she got the best room down at Dog Patch because she was female and it seemed the proper way to do things, she didn't seem to let it bother her too much.

Factor in the fact that Smokey liked to play the fiddle and Katy had her daddy's guitar. Then factor in the fact that Smokey was more or less in charge of what went on in that big house next to his and Angelina's, and there you'll probably find the reason Katy got the top story bedroom on the east side of that house. It was private and of a fair size. All Katy had to do was walk up the stairs after showering and then though the "Flop House." The "Flop House" being the place with a bed on either side of the walkway to Katy's personal abode, which, on occasion, might find occupancy by someone that Marshal Bud deemed not fit to be driving from the Granite Store on a Saturday night.

The Dry

It's a dry place, as the name implies. A welcome place after that constant, drip, drip, drip from the "Decline" down below.

It can get cold during the winter months and there is an electric heater in there to quiet the permeating chill one becomes aware of while walking from the portal towards that heavy wooden door.

It's the place with that heavy wooden workbench you sit on as you eat your bologna sandwiches next to the heavy vice Thor uses when he rebuilds a Jackleg.

It's the place where you divest yourself of your diggers, hang your belt and battery pack on that big nail driven into the wall next to the place you hang your brass. It's the place you hang your hardhat and snap your mine light onto the charger at the end of the shift.

Timothy O'Leary (November 28, 1977)

A bit more of Timothy O'Leary's logbook philosophy, I suppose.

Winter's Snow

Neil Niven, in the year 1880 or around there somewhere. From and interview conducted by William C. Haight for the Federal Writers Project (1939)"

Winter covered the mountains with snow. As soon as the snow started falling the men began an almost never-ending shoveling of drifts from the walks we used in town. Ravines that during the summer harbored laboring miners were completely filled with snow. The houses we lived in looked rather like large Eskimo ice houses.

The mountain streams were beautiful at this time of the year. They cut a sparkling, almost black line through the heavy crusted snow, they were about the only thing in that country that didn't look frozen.

The high drifts, piled higher by changing winds, blocked the trails and entrances to the mines. Often operations were forced to shut down."

It was just those two buildings. You could call it three if you counted the shed in which we put the firewood. It was a big, drafty, two-story house of antiquated vintage, setting next to what looked like a very comfortable looking three-room cottage.

Smokey and Angeline lived in that cottage: bare barn board brown; rusty tin roof; eight paned windows, neatly trimmed in white, and a covered veranda all across the front.

A practical people, to my way of thinking, built Smokey and Angelina's house. It was designed so the heavy winter snows would slide off that tin roof and land at the sides of that house, not in front of the door.

Both of those buildings were built out of heavy mine timber and planking cut in a local mill in the late nineteen twenties, I would wager. The nails that held them together weren't all square, but some were.

When they built it, they (whoever they were) built Dog Patch down in a holler next to some sapling pine. That pine eventually grew to be huge red Ponderosa, and the sun... it never seemed to shine... with exception of a few weeks either side of the summer solstice.

We single miners got to use that big two-story house next door to Smokey and Angelina's place. Home away from home for us it was; that drafty old house with the doors to the side, so that the winter's snows would slide off that rusty tin roof, and block entrance or egress, depending where a person was when those snows slid.

There was a rickety set of three stairs near the back, right near the course of Granite Creek. Stairs that lead into a room that looked like it might have been tacked onto the back of that old two-story house as an afterthought. That "after thought" contained a toilet, hot water and a shower, and those folks in and around that didn't have those things made use of it. *(Kind of an unwritten rule, I suppose.)* Sometimes the bar of soap would disappear. Sometimes there would be a new one. Sometimes the toilet paper roll would be empty.

Sometimes Terry would return the towel he borrowed day before yesterday... or he would want to borrow another one. Everything about Dog Patch got a lot of snow. Granite was not exactly the same elevation as the Anthony Lakes Ski Resort, but the snows were just about as deep.

The county kept the North Fork Highway open as far as Granite – as best they could – but that was about it. If you lived out further than Granite proper you were pretty much on your own as far as getting around in the snow goes.

Kenneth C. Loughton had me leave an old cable bladed D-7 Cat down near where the counties plowing ended and the snow began. Then he gave me the job of plowing the roads as far as the Cougar and Dog Patch.

I said: "Hey Ken, am I going to get paid extra for this?"

And he said: "Free rent… don't complain."

The power to Granite in those days was an iffy sort of affair, at best. Not something a person could really depend on. The power lines to Granite in those days were hanging on poles that often canted off to the side at a forty-five-degree angle; old and broken, filled with holes drilled by woodpeckers chasing timber ants. In a few places a person could see where that power line had actually been tacked to a tree to keep it off the ground and out of the snow. The power could go away for a day, or maybe four.

Those in and around with candles, kerosene lamps, and Coleman Lanterns seemed to get along just fine. They always had. At that time about the only things requiring electricity were few bare light bulbs and receptacles grafted to the ceilings and the walls of those buildings closest to the power lines, and most everything that kept a person warm ran on wood.

Katy Gunn had a red and white Hudson's Bay Jacket; the kind that weighed in at about five pounds; the kind made of heavy wool, and she still never seemed to get warm.

Cecil bought a waterbed, for whatever reason.

The Cougar was an easy-going operation. It was not quite as easy to shut down as flipping a light switch, but it was not all that difficult, either. We had three big switches and they were not all that big as far as switches go. We just tossed a couple of those switches and shut everything down, with exception of those pumps that kept the Decline from flooding, and left for warmer, less snowy, parts of the world from Christmas Eve until the day after the New Year. (1978)

Thor stayed and watched the pumps for us that year. Granite was his home. He lived on the mine's property, and the portal to the Decline was just down the road and around the corner from his house.

I went to Baker City. That was my home.

Katy Gunn went back to "Frisco" in that old Plymouth Valiant that we had to wench out of a snow bank and get running again because she hadn't felt the desire to drive it after the first snow that year.

Cecil went to Baker, then Council over in Idaho, then Boise, then Weiser.

On the evening of the twenty-third of December (1977) it started to snow, and it seemed like it never would quit; big fluffy flakes that floated down like big white fluffy feathers. Three new feet by the second of January, and everything was piled high with fresh, clean, whiter than white, snow. Snow piled high on the limbs of fir, the limbs of pine, the boulders in the creek, and those rusty tin roofs that still made up a goodly portion of the city of Granite.

I started that old D-7 early and I finished late. It was well after dark when I got that rattling beast shut down at Dog Patch. The moon was full, bouncing its light off the snow and I could see most vividly; everything a monotone; everything silver to gray. I could also see the snow had slipped off the rusty old roof of that old two-story domicile those of us were starting to call home when we weren't someplace else. I could also see that there was no way anyone was going to get in there without climbing through a second story window. The entire bottom half of that place was buried and gone.

I sat on that old, cold, steel contraption, quite comfortable, wrapped in a fiber filled snow suit with a heavy fur collar that I'd bought at Bohn's Men's Store down in Baker City the day before. It was then I began to hear the soft rumbling of Granite Creek as it coursed under the snow and ice nearby… all there was to hear.

"Where's Cecil?" was what Katy Gunn said when she pulled up next to where I sat marveling at the wonders of nature.

"I don't know. He'll be along. I see you got some new tires on that old car of yours. Not quite as slippery is it?"

"No, it's not... and I got the heater fixed also... and isn't that hump of snow in front of where the door used to be his pickup?"

"Why, so it is."

About that time there was the flare of a wooden match being lit and the dull glow of a kerosene lantern in a second story window of that old house.

Then Cecil pulled that window open and said "Hello, I'm here."

And Katy Gunn said: "Why so you are. How'd you get in there?"

"I was in here when all that snow slid off the roof. I got a fire going down stairs... for as long as the wood in here last, anyway. I got it pretty warm. That's probably why all that snow slipped off the roof. A good way to get in is to climb up on the shower room and get in through my window."

The power had gone out about the time we left Dog Patch for the holidays. It was still out when we got back. The electricity could have been out to Granite in general, I suppose. Maybe it never got reported to the power company because telephones were scarce and probably went down along with the power. Maybe those concerned figured the electricity would get fixed and running sooner or later, like it always did, so why get all fussed up about it; just the way things were.

When the power went out to Dog Patch the power went off to Cecil's waterbed, and as a result, Cecil's waterbed froze.

When Katy finished crawling through the window to the room Cecil occupied she noticed that bed was the same shape as a big loaf of bread. She gave it a good solid tap with her knuckles as she walked by. That bed sounded like it was filled with wood rather than water.

"Maybe you shouldn't have bought a water bed, Cecil. That bed is going to be really uncomfortable."

Big Ben

Big Ben was one of those big brass alarm clocks with a heavy, hand-wound, "Tick Tock... Tick Tock... Tick Tock."

Big Ben was an alarm clock with brass hammer that would bang on big brass bells until the springs that powered that clock wound down to nothingness if you didn't reach your hand from under that heavy, warm, sleeping bag and push the little leaver that would pin that hammer against one of those brass bells, stopping Big Ben's infernal wakeup call.

Big Ben is telling you that it's time to get out from under that lovingly warm sleeping bag and put your timid bare feet on that cold linoleum floor; that cold linoleum floor in that room with a spider's web of frost on the window, inside and out.

And so, the Day Shift begins. You have forty-five minutes to get the preliminaries out of the way and get down that icy road to the part of that Day Shift that pays you for your time. You have only forty-five minutes instead of an hour because you dallied under the warmth of those covers debating whether the whole thing was worth the hassle or not.

It's time to pull those wool socks over your cold feet. It's time to pull those stiff cold pants and that heavy wool shirt over the thermal underwear you sleep in and step down the stairs.

Katy Gunn would be sitting on a stool in front of that propane camp stove intensely watching a coffee pot perk. (*As if banging the side of that pot with a spoon is going to make the coffee brew any faster.*)

Timothy O'Leary would be standing beside that stove pulling his trousers over his wool underwear; the kind of underwear that a person would see old men wearing in the western movies of the time; the full body length wool underwear with the trap door in the back.

Timothy said that "Union Suit" was a little itchy, but it was easier to get used to that itchiness than it was to get used to being cold most of the time.

It's time to open the door on that old potbellied stove and toss in a few sticks of wood: a few sticks of Larch; on top of those a chunk of Beetle Kill Pine; then a Chunk of Fir. Close the door and open the draft; see if you can get the fire to move a little faster.

When Cecil gets in from his Graveyard Shift, he will bring in an armload of wood and stoke that fire again before it goes out. You're almost sure of that. He'll have the chill leftover from that Graveyard Shift in his bones, and that stove is a good place to linger when all there is to look forward to from the outside world is cold, and getting colder, with each passing day.

It's time to take the Company Mantrip's battery from behind that stove where it's often nice and warm. It's time to take that battery through the door, down the steps, through that berm of crusty snow plowed up in front of the Company's Mantrip, set that battery under the hood and tighten the pole clamps with freezing fingers and that eight-inch crescent wrench in your back pocket.

Last night's Denty Moore beef stew. Last night's Sloppy Joe mix on a warm piece of toast. If there was nothing else, cold Fruit Loops cereal and cold milk.

That was breakfast. Baloney, slathered with mustard and mayonnaise, between four pieces of day-old bread tossed in a paper bag. That was lunch.

When the three of us – Katy Gunn, Timothy O'Leary, and I – walked through the door of the Dry, there would be Jim and Alice. Jim eating his Tuna on Rye breakfast and Alice pouring hot coffee into the mugs held out all around.

And so that Day Shift begins; least ways that part of the Day Shift that pays you for your time and labor.

"You start at the portal and walk down the Decline. There is ice on the airbag, and the fan is very noisy. The farther down you travel it starts to feel a little warmer. The airbag thaws and the fan's noise begins to subside. All you can hear, with exception of some hissing air in the distance, is the sound of your boots on the floor. Then you're at the face. It's an even sixty degrees. It never changes, day or night, winter or summer: sixty degrees. You get a little moist from the water that is constantly dripping out of the Back; that can't be avoided. If you stop moving you get cold, but you won't freeze. Going the other way – traveling out, instead of in – it gets colder, then colder still. Then you step out of the portal, hurry into the Dry, put your light on the charger, hold your hands over the heater a bit, and then get in the company's mantrip for the ride back to Dog Patch and the comfort of that stove."

That was Timothy O'Leary's writing in the logbook that day. February, 15, 1978.

Go away, go away, you cold north wind

Blowin' my muffler 'round and 'round
Your white powder blows coverin' up the icy ground
I'm a slippin' and a slidin' down this dead end
stream
Like a sheep who is lost from the fold
I've been on the land and I've been on the sea
I ain't never seen a night so cold

Suddenly a face at the window
Looks like someone I might a seen before
Thought it musta been my imagination
When suddenly she opened up the door "
And I never expected to see you again
Must a been seven years ago
Now that you're here, why don't you come in.

Russell Smith (1970)

A Pot Belly Stove

Dog Patch was warm on the inside where we sat; Victor, Marlene, Little Lola, and I. The world outside was cold.

"No clinkers... just ash." As Victor opened the door on that antique wood burning stove.

"Red fir is the best. I'm thinking pine would be the next. Tamarack makes good kindling... splits easy... burns hot... and fast." As Victor took that heavy iron poker and lifted a burning piece of wood to look underneath.

Victor had taken over the responsibility and prestigious title "Keeper of The Fire". A duty he assumed when he, Marlene and Little Lola parked that tiny camp trailer next to the stairs that lead to the outside door of the shower room.

It was also one of Victor's unassumed but very necessary duties, to shovel the snows from those outside steps that lead to the shower room and toilet so Marlene and Little Lola could get in and out of that facility. He shoveled those steps so that Marlene and Little Lola could get in and out the lavatory – if you wanted to call it that – without having to walk all the way around that big, old, two-story house on a cold winter's night.

A sooty black stove left over from the turn of the century it was. A wood burning stove left over from a time when stoves were very ornate, and very inefficient. This one stood on cast iron eagle's claws, potbellied and tall, with a sheet of mica in the center of an ornately scrolled door so a person could see the red of the coals glimmering in the firebox when the door was closed.

"No clinkers... just ash." Victor looked at me when he said that.

When the north wind blew between those mountains on either side of Granite Creek the shower room got cold as could be when the hot water in that shower was turned off. It always seemed about then that Old Man Winter's icy hands were most likely to push those towels stuffed under the outside door aside and feel their way along that already cold linoleum floor.

"Just ash – no clinkers." To no one in particular.

It was then that Timothy O'Leary walked in from the shower room, wrapped in a towel, and a stood next to the warmth of that stove brushing his teeth.

Marline was a whole bunch shocked, for she and Victor were from a place other than Santa Barbara. They came from a place where it was very unlikely to see anyone walk into the room with a towel wrapped around his waist and start brushing his teeth, except maybe immediate family... maybe.

"I hope he doesn't drop that towel." If Marline would have said anything that would have been what she said.

Victor and Marline didn't know Timothy O'Leary. They knew who Timothy O'Leary was, but that was about it. They didn't know that Timothy O'Leary was rather casual individual and sometimes things just happened.

Then Timothy sat down on the end of the couch next to Marline and opened a book he'd been showing an interest in. He read for a bit then turned to Marline, who was scrunching up closer to Victor, stuck his finger on the paragraph he'd just read and said, "He just went off and left his wife and children back there in the Dustbowl and hopped a freight headed west."

That stove was a community gathering place, for it was the only source of heat in that big, drafty, old house.

During the summer months folks just sort of went about their own business and that stove seemed a little lonely, sitting there cold, dusty and quiet; gradually filling with used paper towels and paper plates. But during the winter months it was worshipped like some great pagan god. An altar bowed down to by the subservient and the needy; pampered and fed a continuous feast of pine, larch and fir.

There were those that rose in the morning and offered sacrifice before they went to work. There were those that got home from work at seven in the morning and rose in the afternoon to feed that beast. There were those that rose in the middle of the night to stoke that warmth, and if there were no one near of official capacity Smokey or Angelina, from that very cozy little house right next door, would see the duty done.

All around that great pot-bellied stove:
Wet coats and coveralls hanging on nails driven into
the walls,
Or draped over the backs of rickety wooden chairs.
Socks, draped over a strand of cotton cloths line:
hanging, steaming, and drying.

101

Rapid Advance

"….. Rapid advance requires a "high degree of organization… precision in performing the several operations in the work cycle… A breakdown at any point in the work cycle is apt to disorganize the entire job and increase cost…"

Peel's Mine Engineer's Handbook (1917)

Jim and I were trying to get a cap lifted into place. Victor and Cecil had the legs stood when Jim and I started our shift, so getting the cap set on top of those legs and getting the rest of the timbering done was our job. The Back wasn't high enough. There was a big chunk of rock we couldn't bar down hanging where the Cap needed to go and that Cap wasn't going to fit. We needed just a few inches and we didn't have those few inches.

I think we already knew that, but sometimes a person can get lucky…sometimes.

Sometimes abusive verbalization helps.

"Get in there… you son of a bitch!"

And then, all at once… there was George. It was as if he wasn't there, and then he was. Under that hundred and fifty-pound Cap, pushing, heaving and ranting like the two of us.

"Get in there, you son of a bitch!"

My first impression was that of a Ferret; intense and weasel faced. A Ferret with a shiny white plaster cast that ran from the tip of his toe to his hip.

A shiny new plaster cast getting splattered with black mud.

"Why don't you bust that Doney out with a hammer?"

"The hammers in the mucker bucket."

"Who's the mucker operator?"

"Katy Gunn."

"Where is she?"

"She's a little slow getting out of bed this morning. She'll be along in a bit."

"Use the drill."

"The drill's leg's broke… like yours.… And who are you?"

George was a little irked. "I'm the boss."

Kenneth C. Loughton was the first person that I knew of as boss, but he was not around but every so often. He would fly into the Baker City Airport, stick around for a few days and then his other duties would call him away and he would be gone. Apparently, Kenneth had hired George to supervise the Cougar and did not tell anyone. If he did, whoever he told didn't tell Jim or I.

George was stumping back up the Decline, swinging his left leg way out because he could not bend the knee, when Katy Gunn was coming down with the mucker. She stopped and offered him a ride back up that decline in the mucker bucket. She should have headed to the face so that the work could proceed but we didn't worry too much about that sort of thing at the time. Instead she stopped and offered a ride to a stranger in the bucket of a mucker. Everyone knew you weren't supposed to hitch rides in a mucker bucket, but then there are always exceptions to a rule depending which way you want to bend it, and Katy didn't know that this individual was the boss. She was just being magnanimous to a crippled gentleman in a cast who, for some mysterious reason, was making his way up her Decline.

"Want a ride?" was Katy's question.

"Yeah." was George's terse reply.

When George asked katy why she was late: "I'm having trouble with my alarm clock." Katy needed a reason and that was the one she offered.

"Well, you'd better get that problem solved." Was the reply that George offered.

Then George opened the door to the dry and saw Alice. "Who are you?"

"I'm Alice," was her timid reply.

"What do you do around here?"

"I'm with Jim."

"The guy I just saw on the Face?" As George stumped into the dry with the thump and bang of his cast on the hard wooden floor, and started hanging his light on the charger.

"I think so."

"I see." As George began getting the idea how things worked around the Cougar.

Katy Gunn survived her first encounter with George. Apparently, Katy was willing to give up some of her feminist ideology and submit a little more of herself to a world ruled by men due to the fact she needed to send money back home to Frisco, for reasons at that time undisclosed, and the fact she had become fairly comfortable with the way things were going and didn't seem to want to go much of anywhere else right then.

I think that Granite started to boom a little bit more when George became the boss. There were about six more people working at the Cougar after he took over, so I guess that you could say the population of Granite increased by about six.

Some of those that were there before George took their leave; those that did not like strict schedules and that sort of thing just kind of moved on.

Those of us that had gotten used to more strictured surroundings, such as jerking green chain in the mills around that part of Oregon, had a little less trouble adapting to George's set of firm rules. Rules regarding such things as getting out of bed, getting to work on time and not taking a half hour nap after the lunch break.

It was then that the paychecks started to be more official looking. They came with stubs listing deductions and such. Those checks looked a little less like the checks a person would write to buy groceries back in 1978, and they were a little less apt to raise the eyebrows of the bank's teller when we tried to cash them.

The banks down in Baker City did not like to cash those checks anyway. Mostly because they were written on a bank they had never heard of in Colorado. A phone call had to be made to that bank to see if that check was going to bounce or not on a phone that had to be connected to those on the other end by pushing buttons, one at a time. That and the fact that most of those wanting to cash those checks wanted "cash" and weren't too interested in opening a checking and savings account.

However, adaptations had to be made if a person wanted something other than a piece of paper that the local financial institutions regarded as a nuisance. Checking and savings accounts were opened and many of us found ourselves well on our way to becoming regular citizens.

(Sonny still hadn't learned to trust banks. He carried his life savings in a leather pouch in the pocket of his jacket and paid for everything in cash money.)

I was walking through the shop on my way to George's new office in the back, and I couldn't help but notice that Sonny and Thor were having a bit of a dispute; a dispute punctuated by the clatter and bang of Thor heaving his tools into the bed of his pick-up.

Sonny and Thor were involved in a disagreement over who was going to use the shop.

Sonny had gotten into the habit of using that shop to service and work on his Jeep.

Sonny: "I don't ask for nothing to do this. I use my own vehicle to get those kids down there so they can catch the school bus."

Thor thought that the shop was his alone now that George had officially made him a fulltime mechanic, and he didn't want Sonny's personal effects, things like his Jeep and the neighborhood children, cluttering the place up.

Thor: "That's the best way to get things done. Out of the back of a pick-up. That's the best way." As he tossed a set of end wrenches into his pickups bed.

I was looking over my shoulder and listening to that goings on when I opened the door into George's office. He was sitting at his desk with his hands folded in his lap, what was left of his battered cast cocked off to the side and sticking out in the middle of the floor, staring blankly at his new pocket calculator.

(*One of those calculators just after the slide rule and a ways before those that you could actually put in your pocket.*)

"Hey George, what's going on?"

"I'm trying to figure out how to work this thing."

"I mean with Sonny and Thor."

He gave me that exasperated look he would get when things weren't going quite the way he'd anticipated. Like maybe he didn't want me to ask that question.

"Don't!" Was all he said.

I guess it took a while for those of us at the Cougar to get used to the way things had changed since George's arrival. I guess it took a while for those affected to realize that we were actually involved in a business and things needed to go a certain way. George explained that in no uncertain terms. He said "We are either going to be here, or we aren't," and, "We aren't doing so good." It had become perfectly apparent that things were going to require a "high degree of organization" and that idea, in and of itself, took a little getting used to.

This from an interview – conducted by Walker Winslow, December 9, 1938, for the Federal Writer's

Project – with William Huntley Hampton who would have been thirty years old in the year 1900.

"Most of the gold in Oregon has been taken by a man with a gun and dog. I mean that it has been individual enterprise. Most of our mining won't stand the cost of industrial investment, and it has been singularly hard to get anyone to invest in legitimate mining."

"The wildcatters have done well, however.

Mining doesn't work on a pay as you go basis unless you have some extraordinary property, and most of the surface gold that would allow that was taken long ago. I operated at Placer, Oregon, in the 'nineties, on an almost pay-as-you-go basis. But that was placer, and as soon as we got a ways from our water we were up against investment to get our original investment out of the ground. That is usually the story of the shoestring mining. We finally had to sell some of our best property to the Greenback Company, and since they had money they cashed in on our work. I was their superintendent, and so you see it wasn't a matter of what you know or didn't know."

Harley's Wreck

It was a Friday night... Graveyard Shift, and Jim, Katy Gunn, and I were trying to finish a round and get it out of the way. We had that round shot, mucked and timbered and it was looking like we were going to get to take a weekend off. Something we dearly wanted to do.

It had been in near three weeks of bad ground. Not something we could walk off and leave. The ground we were in was not going to let us do that. We had already lost the Face once. We had to back off, retimber, go around, and chances were very good that the Face would have been lost again if we didn't stay after it; three shifts, twenty-four hours a day, seven days a week. That is just the way things were.

We were in one of those clay dikes. A contrary, obstinate, soupy wet mess that was more inclined to fall than let us proceed.

We had taken a short round and gotten lucky. We caught this one just right, and there was a very good chance we were going to get the ground stabilized and get the weekend to ourselves.

We were way ahead of ourselves that night.

What should have taken eight hours had only taken five. We were better than halfway done timbering when the mine phone went off. It was an out of place noise heard above the rattling noise of Katy Gunn's idling mucker more than louder one.

It was Marshal Bud whistling into the handset of the underground phone as loud as he could.

(That was standard procedure for that type of mine phone. A person on one end would whistle as loud possible into the handset and hope it was heard by whoever might be hanging around by the mine phone speaker on the other.)

"Harley's truck is nose down in Granite Creek," is what Marshal Bud yelled into that phone.

It never occurred to any of the three of us that the sun would be up in about three hours to provide the light we might need to see what was going on. What did occur to the three of us was that when the sun did come up it was going to be a weekend, and those of us involved would bust our asses to see that the things needing done got done and we could get good and gone.

Harley had too much to drink at the Granite Store that night and wanted to sleep it off at Dog Patch. Marshal Bud was following him just to be sure Harley made it that far, when something went horribly awry.

Everybody knew Harley was stubborn about most everything. It had to go his way or it just wasn't going to go. However, even he had to admit his home in Greenhorn was too far away from Granite on those muddy twisty roads that night. As it turned out, even Dog Patch, just a little way down the road, was also too far away for Harley that night.

He had gotten his old pickup off the road on the high side, hit a stump, and gotten flipped around in some inexplicable manner. He had managed to weave his way down the slope, through the boulders and trees, and then arch that old yellow pickup, purchase at the county auction two years earlier, quite gracefully it seems, into Granite Creek.

110

Harley was sitting in the Marshal's Scout with a knot on one side of his head and a bloody rag on the other when we got to the scene of Harley's predicament to see what might be needed in the way of tools and equipment.; to see what we could actually do to get him out.

Harley was born in the year 1942. He and Sonny were third cousins, or something of that nature, by way of great Grand Parents that bore the same last name. Sonny was eleven years older than Harley.

When they were younger they would wrestle and Sonny would give Harley a noogy. Harley would go into the house and tell his grandma that Sonny was picking on him. Then Sonny would stick his head through the door and say he was sorry, and Grandma would tell Harley to quit his crying and go back outside and play.

Harley was conscripted into the army in the year 1967. He was twenty-five years of age, the cutoff age for conscription at that time. He served two tours of duty in Vietnam.

He left the military in 1970 at the age of twenty-eight.

He found Darleen (Dar) shortly thereafter, selling bisque ware pots at the Carroll County Fair. Darleen was the daughter of a farmer named Charley Main, who had the place down the road from Harley's grandma. Harley had known Dar nearly since the day she was born.

Darleen was a lot like Harley in many ways: stubborn, intractable, and argumentative. She had already been married and divorced from a man named Bobby White from Kansas City while Harley was in Vietnam.

Dar didn't want to get married again, and she told Harley that in no few words when they first started seeing each other. Harley liked that idea. Then they got married on the second of February 1972.

Harley was restless and Dar didn't seem to mind. Harley seemed to want to be someplace other than where he was, and that was also fine with Dar. They started moving west, no small piece at a time, eventually finding their way to a place called Sumpter out in Oregon in the year 1974, then a place called Greenhorn in 1976.

Harley and the remains of his pickup found their way into Granite Creek in early March of the year 1978, just as that creek was beginning to rise with the early spring runoff. It was a muddy wet time; green grass tossing a white winter's snow aside. That old growth poplar putting forth timid buds, testing the air, not wanting to be fooled again into believing that the spring of the year had actually arrived.

It would have been interesting to see the paperwork Marshal Bud had to do. It would have been interesting to see how the Marshal tried to write down on the necessary paperwork what Harley's truck and Harley had accomplished... if Marshall Bud did any paperwork on the matter at all. It would also have been rather interesting to know what Dar's thoughts were when Marshal Bud gave her, and anyone else that may have been listening, a call on the CB radio about what was going on with Harley and why he wasn't home.

Getting Harley's truck out of Granite Creek took a little innovative thinking and the heavy tools close at hand. The task took our lights to see, a heavy winch on the back of a D-6 Cat, extra cable, and two snatch blocks anchored with chain wrapped around boulders and trees; pulling this way and that... and we finally got his truck back up on the road.

It looked like some sort of aristocratic pig, Harley's truck did. The grill and the front end were pointed up to the sky in a rather snooty fashion. That truck would still start and run, but prudence and the fact that it was nearly daylight and time to begin the weekend's festivities dictated that we tow him to Dog Patch, just to make sure he got there.

When George came on to the mine site that Saturday morning he could see that things weren't quite the way he'd left them the day before. And he asked: "What's going on?" And we told him. Then he asked:" Where's Harley?" And we told him Harley was at Dog Patch with a knot on his head. Then he asked if we'd gotten done what needed done, and we told him that it was. Then he asked "Where you going?" and Katy Gunn said: "Why it's the weekend boss; it's been a long time; we're headed to town."

Angelina got tired of it; all that wrenching and banging; all the cussing. Harley had been at it for about three days. Harley would have Pat drop him off on his way back from the Buffalo in the morning

113

and he'd work on his truck tell about three in the afternoon – pieces and parts, a puddle of oil, and a lot of bad words – when Dar would come down from Greenhorn to pick him up.

Angelina told Harley she would appreciate it if he would take it somewhere else. She basically told him that he was upsetting the serenity that she enjoyed and the slumber of those that had the Grave Yard Shift. Then she told him even she could see that his transportation was a lost cause.

Harley had just about accepted what was blatantly obvious anyway, standing there with a black eye and a one of those Big Patch Band-Aids on his head. It was just that he didn't want to admit that his inebriated transgression was going to force him to part with some of those dollars he had managed to accumulate and buy another old pickup truck.

Harley's truck sat at Dog Patch for a while. Angelina did not like that either, so Harley had it towed up to Greenhorn where it became a relic of sorts.

There were a lot of old automobiles and trucks from previous generations in Granite at that time, just kind of setting where they were last parked, rusting away, some full of bullet holes. If those cars were over fifty years old they were quite often thought of as artifacts of some sort.

Then there were those that weren't even thought of at all; mostly just junk.

There was still a lot of old equipment that could legitimately be referred to as mining artifacts back then; sitting in old bone yards, in front of old adits, and out in the dredge piles. Old ore cars with steel wheels sitting out in the weeds; trommels, tuggers, and winch drums; worn out liners and drills, skips, scrapers, and rusted cable;

shovels with blades worn thin and heavy hammer heads needing handles.

I think a goodly portion of those artifacts managed to find their way into a museum down in Baker City. I've seen old mill balls and rusty end dump ore cars down there.

I've even noticed that a few archaic ore cars found their way as ornamentation into a front yard or two around town; filled with soil and planted with red hydrangea and purple pansy.

Sunday Night Bible Study Class

Angelina said that those coyotes had their own voices, and I believe that is so.

If you let them wake you in the middle of those warm and getting warmer spring nights you'd begin to pick up on that. They would be out there in the trees talking to one another.

Of those coyotes it was Joshua that had a growly sort of thing going on. I think it was Mary that talked like an overly rambunctious teenage girl. To everything Joshua said she would have a sharp and nippy reply. Maybe Joshua was her daddy. I'm pretty sure it was Jaddua that said they didn't have to yell all the time. Subtlety and timing were the thing, in his opinion.

I do not actually know how many of those coyotes there were. There might have been just the three, or there might have been six. At times it was hard to tell, with all the yodeling and yelling going on. On those warm and getting warmer nights in late May those coyote calls would often comingle, and if you were to lay back and listen, you could almost hear the rhythm of the song.

The Reverend Paulson was driving his old Dodge Power Wagon down what we called the North Fork Highway after the roads beyond Granite proper had opened up. He was taking the back road from Pilot Rock and Ukiah back to Baker City, for no better reason than to see what was up that way.

It was starting to get dark when he saw Smokey, Angelina, and some of the rest of us sitting on those porches down there at Dog Patch, and he just pulled in and introduced himself.

The Reverend was newly affiliated with the varied congregations scattered along that stretch of road, and I suppose he saw the opportunity of forming another. He spent that Sunday night reclined in an old sleeping bag on Smokey and Angelina's veranda, listening.

Those coyotes put on a good show for the Reverend that night. I think it was the Reverend Paulson that named Jason, Mary, and Jaddua.

Then there was that Spoon Tailed Raven that struck up a friendship, of sorts, with Smokey, Angelina, and then the Reverend. He would show up on a summer's evening, sit on that big branch on that big red pine, and listen to Smokey tuning his fiddle. He seemed to like the humming of those strings. He would try and join in, but humming and squawking were too far apart in the spectrum of sounds and he just couldn't get it down.

Angelina would say "Jayson, Jayson, Jayson" and Jayson would reply, "Caw, Croak, and Caw."

Angelina asked Cecil, Katy Gunn, Timothy O'Leary, and I, over to dinner on that next Sunday night; the night before those Day Shifts, Swing Shifts, and all those Graveyard Shifts, started again. The Reverend Paulson was there, and Cecil, Katy Gunn, Timothy O'Leary and I were entrapped; courtesy of Angelina: Sunday Night Bible Study Class.

Just after he finished sopping up what was left of Angelina's chili with a slice of her nice, warm, heavily buttered bread the Reverend asked if we believed that God created the world and all in it in seven days.

"Was he using a Timex?" That was a cynical sounding Katy Gunn.

"Was he working just Day Shift or was he running around the clock." That was Cecil's reply, as he started laughing and spilled his beer.

The Reverend was more the philosophical sort: "Maybe a billion years was a day to him."

"Maybe he isn't a he, maybe a he's a she." That was Katy Gunn, again.

"Nope... he's a pot-bellied white man sitting up there in the clouds. I seen him." That was Cecil's answer to Katy Gunn. He had finished cleaning up the beer he spilled and gotten another. He was still laughing.

We all laughed at Cecil's and Katy Gunn's rolling commentary until Angelina let it be known that we had to display better manners and took Cecil's beer away.

The truth of the matter was that Genesis, or anything biblical for that matter, hadn't been thought about very much at all, even on a Sunday, until the Reverend arrived.

The Reverend said he had gotten back to his ancestral home in Salt Lake with his mustering out pay in 1958. He said he had driven long haul for the next fifteen years. He also said he had been on the road so often and home so little he and his wife parted ways, and he just kept on driving.

Eventually, he started thinking that even with all that driving he still was not going much of anywhere. He began to think he was just going. He then got the feeling that there wasn't much to hold him to that "going" so he sold his truck for what he could get, and cast his fortunes to the wind. I guess you could say it was that very same wind that blew him by Dog Patch in early June of the year, 1978.

I would suppose the Reverend Paulson had all the appropriate licenses, permits, and whatever else was required of him by regular society. All the paperwork necessary to be a preacher, or a reverend, or whatever he was. He never referred to himself as "The Reverend." That was the title we at Dog Patch hung on him. To be honest I don't even know what he considered himself, but he wasn't hard to get used to.

I think it was Angelina's cooking more than Sunday Night Bible Study Class that brought us together the first couple of times, but we were there, and the Reverend was there, and he only wanted an hour or so. A fair price to pay for an excellent meal, the company of some interesting people, and some interesting stuff to talk about. (People in their twenties will ponder the cosmos and such, and I guess you could say the Reverend was in his twenties in that regard.)

As those Sundays came to pass we learned how to steer the Reverend's sermonizing, if you wanted to call it that, towards the Old Testament; the testament that held our interest the most. The New seemed a little boring by comparison.

119

The Reverend was our Sunday night companion for the next six months; through the summer months and into the month of November when the snows came again and closed the North Fork Highway. The Reverend told us not to expect him until a Sunday night in the spring of the year when the roads were clear beyond Dogpatch and Granite proper.

I was down there in Baker City about a year ago, and I noticed that the old Grizzly Bear Pizza Parlor had been recommissioned as the "Church of the Guiding Light." I couldn't help wondering if perhaps that was the place the Reverend Paulson had finally decided to make his own. He would have been about seventy-seven years old at that time. I'm sure he would have been tired of all that driving.

His entire life had been wheels on the road, in one way or another. Either as a itinerate preacher of the gospel, or driving a truck. He might well feel the need to slow down some. That old pizza parlor seemed about right for the Reverend; a nice holy place that might serve a decent pizza.

Independence

Mrs. Neil Niven: From an interview conducted by William C. Haight for the Federal Writers Project. (1939)

"On July 4, 1862, the notorious Jack Long discovered gold here, and this precipitated a rush. The town was named in honor of Independence Day, on which it was founded. Later, when the Granite towns people petitioned the United States government for a post office the government insisted they change the name of Independence, for there was already a town named Independence somewhere in Oregon. In accordance with the government edict the townspeople voted for the name Granite.

Jack Long was working as a miner on the Gordon claim. The other miners desiring some liquor, sent Jack out with a pack mule to pack in some whiskey. On his way back the heavily loaded Betsey mired down in a swampy, muddy flat. When Jack pulled her out he noticed her mud-caked feet had gold on them. Immediately he sunk a prospect hole that panned 25 cents to the hand. Jubilantly he filed a claim on the land, and when the news traveled a gold rush was started.

This was on the fourth day of July, 1862."

I don't know precisely what the Granite Store of the late nineteen seventies and the early eighties had been in its past life. I don't think it's even there anymore. It may have very well been one of the local saloons back when Granite was actually a city.

You could call it the Store if you wanted. Nearly everybody did. There was Kraft Macaroni and Cheese, lots of canned soup, some loaves of bread, some mustard, and some catsup. There was Dinty Moore beef stew in two-pound cans, and there was a cooler with a little milk for the neighborhood children and quite a bit of cold beer.

Mostly the Granite Store did a double duty.

Besides being a store, it was also Granite's social hub; a good place to go and drink the beer from that cooler when Day Shift ended at three, or the Swing Shift ended about eleven.

The Granit Store had a bar along the south wall that stretched all the way to the back... and it had a jukebox. Lance was in charge of what went on behind the bar, and Willie was in charge of the jukebox. Willie would make the drive all the way from his home just outside Baker City to tend that jukebox.

There was "Heart of Gold" by Neil Young that played quite a bit. Then there was "How Deep Is Your Love" by the Bee Gees hidden back in the corner of that Jukebox somewhere. It wasn't played much because Disco hadn't quite caught on in Granite yet.

Willie also tended a pool table situated on the Granite Store's old wooden floor; a floor that could easily have been a hundred years old. That floor kind of sagged in between the floor joist, just a bit, and made it difficult to maintain a good level on that pool table. However, with the judicious placement of some wooden wedges borrowed from the Cougar Mine, that table was brought to a reasonable facsimile of level for the pool tournament that Lance decided he would sponsor.

Marshal Bud Morrow and I won the Granite Championship Pool Tournament in the early summer of 1978.

When the Granite Championship Pool Tournament began there were seven teams of two in all, which is an odd number, so one team had to draw a by... and a drawing was held before each round... and Marshal Bud and I drew the by each and every time, making us one of the finalists in the Granite Championship Pool Tournament... and neither of the two of us had done much of anything but watch. When our turn came around, Bud missed the seven ball, then Cecil scratched and knocked the eight ball in the corner pocket, which meant that Marshal Bud and I won the tournament, and I hadn't even gotten near that pool table the whole time.

Lance had purchased two pool cues to serve as first prize. The kind pool cue that broke down into two pieces and fit into a soft case. The tip was bent off to the side on mine when I received it for some reason.

Lance threw more than just a few parties at the Granite Store. Sometimes he didn't throw them. Sometimes they just happened.

It was rather amazing how many people were hidden out in those woods during that particular time in Granite history; people living in little trailers on old placer claims; some just living wherever there was a place to live. Then there were those of us working at the Cougar just down the road and living in a place the locals liked to call Dog Patch.

123

Willie's Jukebox

It sets over in the corner by that old wooden door in the Granite Store, Willie's Jukebox does. The neon lights would flash, the forty-fives would spin.

I've been to Hollywood, I've been to Redwood
I crossed the ocean for a heart of gold
I've been admired by, it's such a fine light
That keeps me searching for a heart of gold
And I'm getting old
Keep me searching for a heart of gold
And I'm getting old

Neil Young (1972)

That jukebox sets next to a bookcase that had become the local library, of sorts. That bookcase that just showed up one day. That bookcase that contained those dime novels, torrid romances, Reader's Digest condensed books, and a copy of "At Play in the Fields of the Lord."

"Bring one in and pick one up." Was the library's loosely run policy.

Sometimes a book would be gone. Sometimes a book would be returned. Sometimes a paper sack filled with Harlequin Romances would find a place. Then there was Tarzan, Conan, and Louis L'amour.

There were two tunes on Willies jukebox that got the most play in the summer of 1978. That melody was "Angel of the Morning." One version by a gal called Juice Newton, another by Marilee Rush.

There'll be no strings to bind your hands
Not if my love can't bind your heart
And there's no need to take a stand
For it was I who chose to start
I see no need to take me home
I'm old enough to face the dawn

Just call me angel of the morning,
Just touch my cheek before you leave me, baby
Just call me angel of the morning,
Then slowly turn away from me.

Chip Taylor (1968)

I guess you could say that Willie had a special interest in that particular jukebox... for whatever reason. There were tunes on that jukebox that weren't considered standard fare for a Jukebox, at that time, in that place.

Those Bill Board Top Forty tunes found on those other Jukeboxes that Willie tended in the Elkhorn Tavern and Cattle Kate's were on Willies Jukebox at the Granite Store, when Willie could find a way to fit them in, but there were others that didn't quite fit the "Top Forty" standardization. "One More Cup of Coffee," sticks in my mind. So does "The Lights of Magdala." "The Weight" was on Willie's Jukebox from the time he had Lance and Thor help him haul it into the Granite Store, just before the first of the year, the winter of 1977.

Willie would be there, at the Granite Store, about three-thirty, on a Friday afternoon, about a half-hour after Day Shift ended, sitting at the bar, with a cup of warm coffee during the winter months, counting quarters.

"Hey, what do you guys want to hear?" When we walked through the door.

Katy Gunn: "Black Crow. That tune by Joanie Mitchell."

"To easy." As Willie flipped Katy a quarter.

Smokey: "I Walk the Line."

Willie:" You might have me there."

Victor: "What you got by the Bee Gees."

Willie: "The Bee Gees… why Victor… I never figured you for a disco man."

"Oh yeah, me and Marlene would go down to the armory back home on a Saturday night… dance all night long."

Sonny, Maggie, and Billy Shortstack; Victor, Marlene, and Little Lola… along with a few cousins, in-laws, and a brother or two had made Granite home by the late June of 1978.

Hillbillies they were… and with them came few pieces of the Blue Ridge Mountains back there in Virginia. One of those pieces a dance called Clogging, and I know for a fact, it can happen, Disco and Clogging can get all mixed together.

"How about a tune by Jackie Lee Cochran." That's what Smokey said he wanted to hear.

Katy Gunn: "I know the one you're thinking of." For, you see, Smokey and Katy Gunn were in cahoots, testing Willies knowledge of the 1950s Rockabilly Blues.

"C-4" Was Willies reply.

126

Well yes now mama
don't you think I know you made a fool of me
My head is hanging low
Lord, you done made a wreck of me
Though you used to say you love me,
it ain't nothing but a lie
You done told me that before and then you left
me high and dry
I don't never want to see you hangin'
'round my door no more

Mama don't you think I know what you done used
me for
Well yes now mama don't you think
I know what you done used me for
Mama don't you think I know
Mama-mama don't you think I know
Mama-mama don't you think I know

Jackie Lee Cochran (1955)

This from Miss Neil Nevin: A citizen of Granite in the late 1800s

"At the Never Sweat Hotel we girls started a library. Every evening we would spend at the library encouraging the young men of the town to read books. Precious little reading was done, but many books were taken out of the library."

"Each girl had a special beau to see that she arrived home safely, but it did not hinder our entertaining the other bachelors at the library."

"The library had the books for an excuse for the miners to come to the hotel, but an old organ helped provide the *entertainment. We would dance and sing to the music of that old, out of tune organ, and have the best time.*

There were four young men there: Mr. Niven, Mr. Butridge, Mr. Tabor, and Mr. Ditmar, who could sing quite well. They developed quite a reputation as the Granite quartet.

Games were popular too, as a form of amusement at the hotel. One game I remember quite well was called "So Very Low." This is a card game played today under the name of "Solo".

"The books in the library were the current novels of the day, although "current" is stretching it aways because current books to us meant a book that had been published within three years of the time we read it. Too, the usual classics were there, although read only by a few of the more studious people."

Little Wing

Smokey was born in 1916. That would have made him sixty-one or two years old in 1977 when we first met. It was Smokey that showed me how to run a jackleg drill and showed Katy Gunn how well her daddy's guitar would sound with his fiddle if she didn't hit the strings too hard.

"You act like you got to run over the top of everything trying to make your daddy's guitar heard. Take it easy... join in, and find a fit."

Then he taught Katy Gunn a tune from when he was twenty years old.

Smokey got his first and only fiddle while hitchhiking back to California from a man with a family of four named Charles Danby who's old flivver pick-up truck had broken down just west of the California Nevada border in 1936.

Smokey was then arrested for hitchhiking and vagrancy, taken back to the California Nevada border and told to go back where he came from, which was his intention in the beginning.

It was the same year he found his way back to that little town and the groves of citrus being swallowed up by that fast growing city to the north and ask Angelina to go with him. That was the same year that he played Angelina the first tune he ever learned on that very same fiddle.

Oh, I got plenty o' nuttin'
And nuttin's plenty for me
I got a gal, got my song
Got Heaven the whole day long

129

No use complaining
Got my gal, got my Lawd
Got my song.

Du Bose Heyward / George Gershwin / Ira Gershwin
(1937)

Katy learned that tune while sitting on that lodgepole handrail that ran around Smokey and Angelina's veranda in that place we called Dogpatch. She learned that tune during those warming and getting warmer evenings after the Day Shift's end; during the muddy, wet, month of May, 1978.

Then Katy Gunn turned Smokey on to the lyrics of a tune called "Little Wing" when the leaves on that old growth Poplar down Granite Creek a ways began to yellow in the early fall of that same year. She wrote those words on the back of one of those napkins that Lance used as coasters up at the Granite Store while we sat at the table having the end of Swing Shift beer.

Well she's walking through the cloud
With a circus mind that's running round
Butterflies and zebras
And moonbeams and fairy tales.
That's all she ever thinks about

Riding with the wind.
When I'm sad, she comes to me
With a thousand smiles, she gives to me free
It's alright she says it's alright
Take anything you want from me, anything.

130

Jimmy Hendrix (1967)

Timothy O'Leary hummed a bit of it.

"Say… that's pretty good." That is what Smokey said as he looked at Katy's writing on that napkin. "That's what you kids listen to these days, is it... Is he talking about his guardian angel?"

Katy smiled at that, and being called a kid, and I'm quite sure Timothy O'Leary had a whimsical thought or two about what would happen when Smokey and Jimmy Hendrix met.

It was then Smokey went over to Willie's Jukebox, adjusted his reading spectacles on the end of his nose, and began thumbing through the tunes on that jukebox with a crippled index finger. He found "Little Wing" on the "B" side of an old "Derrick and the Domino's" forty-five leftover from 1971, and dropped in the quarter that Angelina handed him.

As he came back and sat down he waved that same dirty bent finger at Lance to turn that jukebox up, for you see, Smokey's ears had been exposed to a lot of loud noises over the course of his sixty two years.

I don't think Smokey really cared for the way the tune was carried; with the electric guitars and such, but I'm pretty sure he heard something he liked. Then he looked at Katy Gunn and said, "Let's try that one on fiddle and guitar."

Smokey had been "Bush" nearly all his life. "Bush" – his word – meaning he was never very close to civilized society.

The war years had passed him by. He was a miner of copper in Colorado, and war needed copper worse than it needed Smokey.

Smokey and Angeline's exposure to the world outside was minimal. Other than traveling through the nineteen forties town of Denver every so often, and what was written on those coarse paper pages of the "Rocky Mountain News" Smokey's life was pretty much Smokey's.

"Move it a little to the right... Little more... Good, right there." That was Smokey sighting down the timbers in the rib line to make sure the leg I was wrestling around was set according to his standards.

I had screwed up, to put it quite simply. I had shot out four sets of timber and put everything behind three and a half shifts. Other than the fact that those timbers had to be mucked-out, and replaced, I also had to endure all the bedeviling, chiding, and crass remarks form my coworkers and colleagues about how I had mucked up the next paycheck.

Smokey said, "There are two kinds of miner... Those that have shot out four sets of timber... and those that are going to."

Angelina said she wanted Smokey to give it up, but I don't think either one of them ever considered a thing called retirement a soon to be reality. They were just going to keep going, trying to find a place to fit, and I would suppose that cozy little cottage down there in Dogpatch seemed a good fit, at the time.

Smokey was a sixty-two-year-old man working with twenty-year-old men, and a woman named Katy Gunn in 1978.

Smokey never seemed to move to fast or expend anywhere near the energy we young men did, even if we were involved in the same task.

He never humped any timber and stood a square set, we did all the heavy physical work, but things always seemed to go a little smoother when he was around.

Smokey also had a bit of a limp; not much, but a limp, and he had that bent finger. The only finger he seemed to want to abuse.

William C. Dex

William C. Dex was a citizen of Granite Oregon according to the federal census taken in 1880.

Dex was born in the year 1815 in the state of Virginia. He had quite probably traveled the better than three thousand miles between Virginia and the Gold Rush of the eighteen fifties, for he had a son in California the same year the Civil War began back east in 1861.

Dex would have been forty-six years old at that time of his son's birth, when the life expectancy for a miner would have been somewhere in the early to mid-fifties.

Dex was widowed at birth. Charles Ernst Dex, his son, never knew his mother. Dex was father, breadwinner, and mother, in a time when a woman's work was never truly done. In a time when what was canned and put in the root cellar was what got a family through a long cold winter. Back in a time when a miner's boots were quite rare, quite expensive, and needed greasing with whatever was available before the next day came around. Back in a time when one pair of pants was all there were, and the rips and tears needed to be sewn before the start of the next day's shift began.

C.E. Dex was twenty years old and living with his father in the Granite Oregon of the 1880s. He probably did most of the maintenance on the boarding house his father listed as his occupation at the time.

William C. Dex also quite probably availed himself of the affordable and very available

Cantonese help of that time. One of those people could have been the only Cantonese lady in Granite proper at the time. A girl that Dex called Toy Mavy, seventeen years old, and the only female out of an oriental population of one hundred seventy-seven.

This from a Canyon City interview with a lady only known as Mrs. Ford conducted by William C Haight for the Federal Writers Project. (1939)

"Perhaps the most noted hell-raiser in the history of Canyon City was Marie St. Claire. The wildest, toughest, and most beautiful light woman the houses there ever had. Marie was kind and generous to everyone. If crossed, though, she could draw and plug her man with the best of them. I remember that she would go horseback riding in men's clothes; something no lady, scarcely a light one, would do. When she dressed in her gorgeous velvet dresses, she could dazzle anyone. Marie lived extravagantly. Her home had every luxury known to the world at that time. Her silver service was particularly beautiful. Wild, beautiful, dangerous Marie St. Claire had the secret admiration of everyone, despite her profession."

"Well, I remember it all very well lookin' back
It was the summer that I turned eighteen.
We lived in a one-room, run-down shack
On the outskirts of New Orleans.

We didn't have money for food or rent
To say the least we was hard-pressed
When Momma spent every last penny we had
To buy me a dancin' dress.

135

Well, Momma washed and combed and curled my hair,
Then she painted my eyes and lips.
Then I stepped into the satin dancin' dress.
It had a split in the side clean up to my hips.
It was red, velvet-trimmed, and it fit me good
And standin' back from the lookin' glass
Was a woman
Where a half-grown kid had stood.
She said, "Here's your last chance,
Fancy, don't let me down!
Here's your last chance,
Fancy, don't let me down.
Be good to the gentleman, and they will be good to you.

Bobby Gentry (1970)

The Slot

Granite isn't all that much higher in elevation than Sumpter. I guess it just seems that way. Sumpter is about 4400 feet while Granite is only a couple hundred feet higher, a little better than 4600, as I recollect.

The road leaves Sumpter and angles up a little at a time until it reaches what we used to call the Third Loop Road, and then it gets busy and climbs to about 5700 feet. Up until this time it's called the Granite Hill road and it was a twisty affair indeed. For some reason the folks in charge of naming roads starting calling it the Bull Run Road from that point on.

The Bull Run Road ran along a plateau of sorts for a little way before it dropped down into Onion Gulch at about 4100 feet.

During the summer months that road was a dusty, pot-holy, wash-boardy, wheel-busting affair... but this little tale doesn't have a whole lot to do with the summer months.

There was a place where that road could have been tunnel but wasn't. It was a place where the road cut through the side of Grays Peak in such a way that there was a rock face close in on both sides and open sky high above. Hence its name, and its title, to those of us that came to know it well... "The Slot"

During the winter months, when the snows started getting deep and the county started plowing the winter's snows out of that road, the blade man often had a bit of difficulty with that piece of what we called the North Fork Highway.

The snow had to be pushed somewhere, but there was no place in the Slot for that snow to go. The blade man just kept pushing it off to the side, the road getting narrower and narrower, the snow on the sides of the road getting deeper and deeper, until there was just a one-lane thoroughfare, looking for all the world like one of those bobsled runs that you would see in the Winter Olympics.

It was a Saturday morning in the late winter, early spring, of 1978. The sun was shining bright and warming things a bit; melting a little of the snow and putting a little film of water on the road.

Those of us young and rambunctious wanted to get down to Baker City, with its warm civilization; with its nightlife, conviviality, television, beer, and comfortable beds.

And the road is narrow, sloping to the east, and so slick that a person would simply fall on their ass getting out of their vehicle to look down the Slot while wondering what to do. You couldn't see around that corner down there.

On this Saturday morning, the first automobile to come along was Terry's 1965 Ford Galaxy 500, with the heavy treaded snow tires on all four wheels, carrying Terry, Cecil, and I.

This would have been Terry's third winter up in those parts and he knew about the Slot and its eccentricities. He also knew that when he started down through that Slot he wasn't going to stop no matter what kind or tires he had on the vehicle. He also knew that there could very easily be another vehicle around that corner, so he just pulled us over and waited for the rest of those going down... and the solution to the problem.

The next in line was Katy Gunn in that battered dilapidated Plymouth Valliant, followed by a heavy, antiquated Dodge Power Wagon left over from a military auction held in 1972. A 1940s vintage army ambulance with heavy cleated tires and a set of heavy-duty tire chains draped across a heavy steel pumper driven by Frank Weaselhead.

Frank Weaselhead was a Crow Indian from a place called Lodge Grass up in Montana, and he had a live-in lady companion he called Nightwind.

Nightwind's real name was Beverly.

Beverly was a disillusioned debutant. At least that is what she told me. She said her previous name, the name she had before Frank rechristened her Nightwind was Hussy, and the aristocrats in her age group were rather malicious in their whispers and their teasing. She also said that she didn't like the idea of doing what her parents had dictated she do, what with the debutant ball, the cotillions, and that sort of thing. She said that her life was too enclosed. Things were to well directed and contained, and she didn't like that. She was supposed to marry a man pretty much chosen for her and she didn't like that idea either, so she loaded a suitcase with cloths, slung a sleeping bag over her shoulder, and headed west while no one was looking. It was a rebellious time back then and she wanted to be part of it.

She was hitch hiking through Montana on her way to San Francisco when Frank picked her up in a 1954 Ford Pickup with a cracked window.

By the time Beverly's parents found her it was too late. She had already decided to make a life with Frank and she had also decided Nightwind was a name that seemed to fit. Nightwind was born in 1948. She met Frank Sheepe Weaselhead in 1970. She and Frank were both twenty-six years old when they found their way to Granite in 1974.

Frank wrapped those heavy cleated tire chains around the front tires of that heavy old military ambulance, while a ruddy faced, long winded, Nightwind donned a pair of skis and began to make her way down the high snow bank to that curve below so she could see to the very end of the Slot.

After Frank had wrestled those heavy cleated chains onto those tires and gotten back into the cab he waited patiently for Nightwind's signal, and when she waved her hand he idled that piece of heavy steel and rubber on through.

Nightwind watched and waited until Frank made it out the other side of the Slot, she then signaled Katy Gun to come on.

Katy's vehicle was quite probably the worst possible ride imaginable for that type of place. It was just too slick on the bottom, and her's was a ride I'm sure Katy Gunn from San Francisco California will never forget. It was sort of like watching that steel ball in a pin ball machine banging and bouncing its way down and around the corner with Nightwind cheering her on when appropriate, and laughing each time Katy kissed the snow-covered banks on her way down.

Next it was Terry's turn, but Nightwind ran her hand across her throat, and we knew what that meant. We knew that someone was about to try making their way up through the Slot, which was not very likely.

We knew whoever it was would try, probably end up sideways in the road, and have to rely on Frank to get them squared away and moving again, but to our luck and amazement it was Thor on an old and antiquated Ski Doo snowmobile; one of the big and clunky originals with one ski on the front and a set of tracks on the back imbedded with steel spikes.

"I see you boy's and Katy are going to town. I guess its Saturday ain't it? The road is starting to bare a little down near the river. Look's like Nightwind is certainly enjoying herself."

When the Slot was clear and the way ours, as Terry was making his way past where Nightwind stood, waving a hearty good day, and wishing us good luck on the rest of the way through. The weather was warming and the feeling for the rest of the day was fine. The air was as clean and clear as it was ever going to get.

Nightwind had removed her coat and tied it around her waist. Her smile was broad, her cheeks were red, and we were going to town.

We would all meet up again down at Cattle Kate's, after the errands were done and Cecil had managed to get the front fender of Katy Gunn's

Plymouth pulled out of the wheel well on the driver's side.

The Road to Cattle Kates

This from an interview conducted by William C. Haight with a gentleman named Charles Imus, a citizen of that part of the world in 1880 or so, for the Federal Writers Project (1939)

"The coach we used was a Through Brace coach, the hardest ridin' coach man ever made. Most coaches were springed up, and they would rock sort of from side to side. The Through Brace's motion wuz a forward and backward one. It made it awful hard ridin'. When you hit a good bump like as not you'd bite a kidney.

Sometimes you'd slip and fall into the boot. Damn, but that would hurt! The Through Brace stagecoach was a much harder drivin' coach. Many times we would have to strap the passengers and ourselves in good and tight to stick with the durn wagons."

"When the roads started getting bad, wuz when our real trouble started. The Through Brace coach would give way to a Democrat and four horses. A Democrat is a skeleton wagon that has a bottom bed and wire rack for a side. A feller could easily lift one end of a Democrat with one hand. Even so, the snow and slush would get too much for the horses to even pull a light wagon like a Democrat. Then the Democrat would go into the barn and we'd have to pack the mail through. Passengers would ride a horse."

These days that road is what they call the Elkhorn Scenic Byway. A person can drive from Baker to Sumpter along the Powder River, then

143

from Sumpter through Granite, and from there along the upper reaches of the John Day River, turn east at the Ukiah Junction and head for Anthony Lakes. From there it is downhill to Haines, and from there it is back to Baker along old Highway Thirty.

Essentially you can make a nice comfortable loop behind that granite escarpment east of Baker City they call the Elkhorn Ridge on paved road. Just get on the Elkhorn Scenic Byway and follow it back to where you started...Baker City. You might not even get your car dirty.

In the summer of 1978, the road from Sumpter to Granite was a little wider than it was in 1916. It was cleaned and graded more often, I'm sure of that. I also think the grade on the Granite Hill portion of that road had been lessened quite a bit, but that road was still dirt and gravel, and at times rougher than if there was no road at all.

That road would be wet and soft in the early spring of the year, when what was left of the winter's snows still lined the sides of that muddy road. It was then the general traffic and log trucks would turn that road into yawning potholes, jagged washboards, and cavernous ruts. The county blade would fill in the rough spots every so often, but it never seemed to be enough, and it never seemed to last.

There were two recognized methods for traveling that particular road. One method was to travel as slow as one felt necessary. Ease the vehicle down into the holes, creep out the other side, and hope that certain pieces and parts on the automobile were not twisted in the process. The other method was to

144

go so fast the tires on the vehicle didn't have time to go down into the holes. The idea was to just hit the high spots between the valleys and smooth the ride a little bit. The former method and things just kind of fell apart a piece at a time, the latter method and things just kind of fell apart all at once.

We each had acquired a paycheck, and we were headed to town: Cecil, Katy Gunn, Timothy O'Leary, Terry, and I. You could have seen us coming if you were on that straight stretch of the North Fork Highway before you reached Granite City Limits in July of 1978. You would have seen an old beat-up Plymouth Valliant, a faded, dusty white Volkswagen Beetle, an antiquated pickup truck with its rusty fenders flapping in the wind, and a 1965 Ford Galaxy 500, all headed to Baker City in front of a dusty summer's breeze.

"A caravan of vagabond souls headed to the big city where they are going to cash in their freedom's for car payments."

That would have been Terry's rap, and it'll give you an idea of what his attitude about life in general was. I would be willing to wager that he probably had his first dollar, and a whole bunch of others, buried somewhere out there north of Granite proper in a Prince Albert Tobacco can.

Terry had adapted. He had been driving that road for a while and learned what he did from hard experience. His vehicle was that 1965 Ford Galaxy 500, with heavy-lugged truck tires on all four wheels, and a driving method that looked a lot like the rambling insanity of a madman: accelerator, brake. "Nice and slow through here." Accelerator, brake, accelerator again, "Stay on the left side of the road until that corner up there."

My particular reason for heading to Baker City that day was a clam chowder served at the Inn Land Café. I'd been smelling it for a week in my dreams. I guess I had a craving for something other than Spaghetios for supper and Fruit Loops cereal with cold milk for breakfast.

I was on my way to Cattle Kate's when I walked by Newburger and Hilner's and found those four – Katy Gunn, Terry, Timothy O'Leary and Cecil – standing in front of the window gazing at the televisions on display. They were standing there rather transfixed; kind of bedazzled by the colors, I guess you might say. It had been a while since one of those things had been seen. They were watching a sitcom called "All in the Family" with Archie and Edith Bunker and another person named "Meat Head."

Cattle Kate's could be a rough and rowdy place at times, not all the time, but it could happen, especially when the Pipeliners came to town. Those folks always seemed to be getting into fights, seemingly for no better reason other than for something to do. It was not much different on that night, with the exception of the fact that the bouncer got overworked and gave up, leaving Cattle Kate's bouncerless, when it needed one quite badly.

Timothy O'Leary knew from personal experience about Cattle Kate's and the crowds that would gather Saturday Night. So did Cecil. I think we all did, and for some outlandish reason we might even have been looking forward to a rowdy night on the town.

It would start off… "Easy Enough." Sometimes that "Easy Enough" would last until closing time…sometimes it wouldn't. The evening would start with people sitting around tables and talking, then people laughing and dancing, then a little yelling, then whatever came next.

It would be about then an angry young man, not much more than a toddler with a wisp of a mustache, would stomp down that aisle that ran the length of the bar and out front door, apparently slighted by a woman who could have been his mother standing in the middle of the floor watching him leave with her hands on hips.

That woman was Carrie. She had a redheaded working gal's muscle in a tank top with a little streak of sweat running down the back and a few drops of that same sweat on her forehead.

Carrie owned Cattle Kates, and a goodly portion of the time she was also the accountant, the cook, the bartender – and at times – the bouncer.

Darren was to be the bouncer that night but he had been hired away by one of the pipeline crews and was sitting in one of the corner tables drinking beer with his newfound associates, under Carrie's baleful stare.

It was a busy night… and the band played on.

There was dancing and fighting on the dance floor at the same time that night.

Terry was rolling around on that floor, trying to get away from a big burly dude named Alfonzo.

147

Apparently, they had been bumping butts while dancing, Terry with Katy Gunn and Alfonzo with Suzy Escovel.

Apparently, Alfonzo took umbrage to something Suzy said and gave her a slap on the face, and Terry, being the chivalrous kind, told Alfonzo to knock it off and gave him a shove, with a rattle and a bang from the big bass drum, into the bandstand. I think it was then that Terry realized the error of his chivalry and tried to get away, but too late.

"You guys want to knock it off! I mean it!" That was Katy Gunn.

It was then Katy Gunn tried to grab Alfonzo by his belt so she could pull him off Terry, but she had gotten hold of his briefs instead, and was in effect giving him a bodacious wedgie.

It was also then that Carrie, and Darren, her ex-bouncer, rehired on the spur of the moment with the wave of a hand, intervened with the help of Cecil and Timothy O'Leary, to get Alfonzo out the door and eventually into the back of a police car that had pulled up to the curb.

"Now look, folks… we're a country and western band. That's what we do, but we've been playing the Doobie Brothers and Aerosmith, and now folks are asking us to play disco. Now… we're a country and western band. How about 'Mamas Don't Let Your Babies Grow Up to Be Cowboys.' We do a really good version of that one."

Cowboys like smokey old pool rooms and clear mountain mornin's
Little warm puppies and children and girls of the night Them that don't know him won't like him

And them that do sometimes won't know how to take
him
He ain't wrong he's just different
But his pride won't let him do things to make you
think he's right

Mama don't let your babies grow up to be cowboys
Don't let 'em pick guitars and drive them old trucks
Let 'em be doctors and lawyers and such
Mama don't let your babies grow up to be cowboys
'Cause they'll never stay home and they're always
alone Even with someone they love

Ed and Patsy Bruce (1975)

Katy Gunn and Suzy Escovel were sitting on the bench outside the front door to Cattle Kate's, sharing a large glass of peppermint schnapps, when Timothy O'Leary opened that door on his way to find a motel to spend the rest of the night.

Timothy O'Leary, looking back over his shoulder at the goings-on back in the bar: "It must be nice to lead such comfortable and sedate lives" Then to Katy Gunn: "You don't seem to be too upset by all that."

Katy Gunn, with a little bit of a smile, then a little bit of a giggle: "It reminds me of what used to be my home life... a little."

Cecil bought a new used Scout the next day; a red one with black vinyl seats. It was nice, shiny, and clean... for a while. Then it ended up out its element. (*I think it was a little too asphalt for the part of the world it finally ended up in.*) It was taken up the Granite Hill and filled with dust on the dashboard and mud on

149

the floor. After a while it developed a few squeaks; one here and one over there by the back window, then it blew a tire, or maybe two. Then someone got in on the passenger's side with a screwdriver in her pocket and ripped a hole in the seat. Then the passenger's side door got tweaked somehow and had to be tied shut with a piece of bailing twine, or it rattled like a pan full of marbles... and for some reason it didn't seem quite as red anymore. *(That took about three months.)*

Yeah. Terry had adapted, least ways as much as those rocky mountains he called home were going to let him.

We each had our challenges in the life Granite wanted to offer I suppose; those things that made life uncomfortable at times; those things that would crawl into your boots at night and be waiting to surprise the holy living shit out of you when you wanted to put those boots on in the morning.

But Terry had just a little bit more to deal with than the rest of us in that regard, for chipmunks were Terry's complete and total nemesis.

When he moved into that trailer up above the First Level Portal so did they, for Terry had what they wanted: Tuna fish and cookies; that sort of thing.

He woke one spring morning in 1977 to a nice new batch of little pink chipmunks nestled in a little pink ball in his underwear drawer.

"You think they are really adorable until there are about ten of em. I woke up to one of those fuzzy little devils sitting on my face last night."

KOIN TV

Apparently, in the late summer of 1978, there was not much newsworthy happening in the rest of the world and KOIN TV down there in the Valley needed some time filled.

It was then you would have seen Marshal Bud walking down the main street of Granite Oregon with a young lady named Annalee Rice attentively hanging on his arm, followed by a film crew of three, humping a bulky camera, battery packs, and sound recording equipment.

Bud was giving the quick nickel history tour as he and Annalee walked down that main street with the camera crew in tow. The Marshal would point to a turn of a century building that used to house an apothecary.

"This building was probably built about 1890. Granite wasn't exactly booming then but there were still a few hotels and restaurants along this street here. On that empty patch of ground over there was a hotel that had sixty-five rooms."

Marshal Bud was probably trying to put on a bit of an act; a performance for the Sunday morning patrons of KOIN TV, and Annalee might have seen that the Marshal's performance really wasn't all that much of a performance after all… whether Marshal Bud knew it or not. Annalee may have detected that subtle backwoods Eastern Oregon strum of voice native to the Marshal and those like him, and that, quite obviously, fascinated her.

"That building you see down there is where Otis Ford lived back in sixty-six. He was the mayor back then... the population of Granite was about four."

"At one time there were two newspapers here... back about 1890 or so. I don't know where they were, though. I think the Boulder was right over there. Granite grew up real fast, and then it just wilted away a piece at a time."

The camera operator kept the lens on Bud and Annalee. He seemed to be trying to capture the ambiance of Granite and the Marshal at the expense of those of us sitting in old pickup trucks and standing around in front of the Granite Store watching the proceedings with a captivated curiosity.

One of those captivated was a lean shouldered, sharp featured, woman with short brown hair sitting in a wooden rocker rolling herself a Bull Durum Cigarette.

"Bud seems to be taking quite handily to his newfound notoriety," said Angelina; rocking nice and slow on the creaky wooden floor of the Store's front porch.

"Yup," said Smokey who was sitting on the steps in front of Angelina's rocking chair.

Most of the time, in 1978, Granite was a relatively quiet place. Every so often an old pickup truck would come up Center Street, past that little rusty brown building with the rickety bell tower that used to be a one-room schoolhouse in 1900, or thereabouts.

If that old pickup were to turn right down Main Street it would roll past what was left of those turn of the century buildings that used to be Granite's business district. Past those brown and falling down storefront facades. Past that old dry goods store with what used to be owner's living quarters above. Past that old warehouse with the weeds growing through the freight elevator in the back. Past what was quite probably a boarding house that could have belonged to a man named William C. Dex in times more prosperous. Past a life that used to be. Past a life that hadn't gotten around to letting go completely, just yet.

I don't think that those buildings exist anymore; those buildings left over from the turn of the century; those buildings still standing in 1978. Most have probably collapsed under the weight of their own antiquity. That old dry goods store, or whatever it was – that building Jeremy and his dad called home for a while – is gone. It was a building with a steep tin roof to shed the deep winter's snows behind a square storefront façade. A façade on which C. W. Dagget chose to advertise his wares – "C W Daggett, Boots, Shoes, Hardware, Crockery, Groceries & Liquors" – in big yellow letters. Letters faded, washed out, and nearly gone.

There were a few of the original outhouses left back in 1978, but not many. There used to be as many of those little communal buildings as the near four-hundred people would need in 1870.

Those outhouses had fallen into disuse mostly because the miners of that time had moved on, that and the advent of porcelain and the flush toilet.

Many of those outhouses had been tipped over on Halloweens past. The four-holer was quite probably the last tipped, but not until after someone had painted a yellow dividing line, with lumpy yellow machine paint, down the middle, then "Men" on one side of that line, and "Women" on the other.

I never saw that segment on KOIN TV's Sunday morning show. Quite probably because television didn't work to well in Granite at the time.

I have often wondered about that little segment. I have often wondered what Marshal Bud and Annalee were talking about when they were not talking about the sites and history of Granite.

Stereo

*I*t was late in the day when I walked by May's Music in downtown Baker in the summer of 1978. It seemed like a good idea at the time. I went inside to thumb through the L.P.s and maybe see if I could persuade Chuck to spin that tune I had rolling around in my head. That tune I heard on that scratchy old radio just south of Sumpter as I was coming to Baker City on Highway Seven.

> *Winding your way down on Baker Street*
> *Light in your head and dead on your feet*
> *Well, another crazy day*
> *You'll drink the night away*
> *And forget about everything.*

> *Gerry Rafferty (1978)*

The sign hanging over the door still said "May's Music" even though Chuck was the new proprietor. I guess it was easier to leave the name as what it was rather than change that sign over to "Chuck's Music". Maybe Chuck left it at May's because May's Music carried a more lyrical quality.

This was back in the days when those that fancied themselves audiophiles were into stereos made of components rated in watts… the more, the better.

When I left May's Music that day I had the biggest, heaviest, conglomeration of stereo Chuck had to offer. I had speakers that made good end tables (Still do), an amplifier (Carver System) that weighed in at close to eighty pounds, a high-end cassette tape player, and a "Sound Shaper One" graphic equalizer to make things sound just fine.

I could see Chuck standing on the sidewalk outside May's in my mirror waving goodbye as I pulled away; waving with the check I had written on my brand-new Western Bank checking account between the index finger and thumb of his right hand.

Then I hauled all that up to that drafty old two-story house with the rusty tin roof near the town of Granite. Home for me and a few others… back then.

I guess there was always music, of one form or another, floating around Granite in those days; Smokey's fiddle – easy to get along with. Billy Shortstack's guitar – when she was around; Billy Shortstack and Smokey – soft and easy on the porch across the way; Timothy O'Leary – always whistling and singing in the shower room. Willie's Jukebox up at the Granite Store. Katy Gunn learning to play her daddy's old guitar, whenever she felt like she had to try.

I set that stereo up on a Sunday.

Timothy O'Leary was waiting… anticipating. He pulled a cassette tape he was partial to out of his pocket – first thing – slid it into the tape player, ever so gently and shut the lid, before I could say much of anything.

I can see her lyin' back in her satin dress
In a room where ya do what ya don't confess
Sundown you better take care
If I find you been creepin' 'round my back stairs

Sundown ya better take care
If I find you been creepin' 'round my back stairs

She's been lookin' like a queen in a sailor's dream
And she don't always say what she really means
Sometimes I think it's a shame
When I get feelin' better when I'm feelin' no pain
Sometimes I think it's a shame
When I get feelin' better when I'm feelin' no pain

Gordon Lightfoot (1974)

Smokey and Angelina crossed that little span of grass and gravel between that cozy little house they called home and through the door nearly as soon as they heard that tune. Smokey with a freshly made gallon jug of raspberry wine.

There were about nine of us, gathered around, intently listening to that refined sound, after word of a new stereo in town had been passed around: Smokey and Angelina – Timothy, Katy Gunn, Cecil, and I – Victor, Marlene, and Little Lola… and then the Reverend Paulson made an appearance, as he always did on those warm Sunday nights, rounding our number to an even ten.

"I've got a tune." Is what the Reverend said, as he turned and walked back out the door to get that tune in the tape player he'd grafted into the dash of his old Dodge.

It was Sunday evening. *(Sunday Night Bible Study Class.)*

"You strum away on your harps like David and improvise on musical instruments." That was the Reverend, as he slid his tape into the machine, pushed the "play" button, and stepped respectfully back between the speakers, to achieve the best stereo sound.

Once I had mountains in the palm of my hand
And rivers that ran through every day
I must have been mad
I never knew what I had
Until I threw it all away.

Love is all there is, it makes the world go 'round
Love and only love, it can't be denied
No matter what you think about it
You just won't be able to do without it
Take a tip from one who's tried

So if you find someone that gives you all of her love
Take it to your heart, don't let it stray
For one thing that's certain
You will surely be a-hurtin'
If you throw it all away
If you throw it all away

Bob Dylan (1969)

This from a young Nell Niven, the schoolmarm in Granite Oregon (1880)

"Other amusements that we had were community dances, community sings, and one whale of a big celebration on the 4th of July. You see we not only celebrated the signing of the declaration of Independence but also the founding of our town. The celebration was similar, I suppose, to other small towns; other than the fact that there were so few girls in our town."

158

"At these celebrations, the men that were not courting the girls spent their time and money in one of the several "wet groceries." They would get hell-roaring drunk and gamble their hard-earned money as if it were water."

Oh ladies, oh gemmen, come now wid me
Well dance till de mornin, so sweet and merrily
Were darlings , were dandies,
So elegant and grand,
Keep moving to the music of Paddy Gilmores band.

Ed Harrigan and David Braham (1882)

Mama Wants to Borrow a Loaf of Bread

Katy Gunn was sitting on that lodgepole handrail that ran around Smokey and Angelina's veranda. She was picking at a tune that Smokey wanted her to learn.

Katy wasn't exactly what a person would call a guitar virtuoso by any means. She knew a blues rift of two. She knew most of the cords in the key of C, and she had her daddy's guitar.

G was just fine. D was a little rough. C seemed to fit.

> *"Away by the waters so blue*
> *The ladies were winding their way*
> *While Pharaoh's little daughter went down to the*
> *water*
> *To bathe in the cool of the day*
>
> *Before it was dark she opened the ark*
> *And found the sweet babe that was there*
> *And away by the waters so blue*
> *The infant was lonely and sad*
>
> *She took him in pity and thought him so pretty*
> *And it made little Moses so glad"*
>
> *Carter Family (1929)*

It was Sunday night, the Reverend Paulson had arrived, and Katy Gunn, Cecil, Timothy O'Leary and I were invited across the way for an excellent

Sunday night repast, coupled with Sunday Night Bible Study Class.

We had finished the dinner that Angelina had prepared of chicken and dumplings, or rather a lot of dumplings and a little chicken. Chicken and dumplings made of that old stewing hen that the Reverend had brought along in a cardboard box in the back of his old Dodge Power Wagon.

An elderly lady named Rose Marie that lived on a back road near Pilot Rock had given him that old hen, still kicking and curious about the ride, instead of a five-dollar donation to the Church of the Guiding Light.

When the Reverend finished sopping up the last of Angelina's dumpling sauce with the last of that warm bread slathered with warm melted butter, the Reverend leaned back in his chair and began.

"Then said the LORD unto Moses, Behold, I will rain bread from heaven for you; and the people shall go out and gather a certain rate every day, that I may prove them, whether they will walk in my law, or no."

Cecil: "What's he talking about?" to no one in particular.

"Don't you feel lucky. Lucky to be where you are and the fine foods we get to eat?" Said the Reverend Paulson, addressing the question to Cecil, while nodding a thank you in Angelina's direction.

"Never thought about it much. I either had it or I didn't." Is what Cecil said.

Billy Shortstack was walking between those big Ponderosa Pine on her way down to Smokey and

Angelina's front porch with her guitar slung over her shoulder when Cecil said that.

"Mama wants to borrow a loaf of bread," Billy Shortstack said. "She wanted Daddy to go to town today and buy a loaf and a few other things, but Daddy doesn't want to go. He said he kept flour around for that purpose, and to make some. I don't think that's working out quite the way he figured. Mama wants to borrow a loaf of bread."

"All we have is homemade." Is what Angelina said.

"Well good, Mama can tell Daddy she made it, and everyone will be pleased."

This from an interview conducted by Manly M. Banister for the Federal Writers Project (1939) with Mrs. J. N. Doane, a citizen near Sumpter in 1890 or so.

"Almost everything people used was shipped in. They raised very little stuff at first because they didn't know they could. Almost everything had to be hauled in from the Umatilla Landing. Sugar came in 100-pound barrels. People had their own beef, and they made their own butter. In later years they found out that the ground would produce, and they began to raise a few vegetables."

"They didn't have as many vegetables, either, it seems like in those days. There were cabbages, apples, potatoes, onions, and beets, and that was about all. No carrots or other vegetables like people have now. I don't know why not."

"Oh yes, there were dry beans, too, and a little canned stuff, but not nearly so much as they have nowadays. There was no such thing then as canned milk. People bought lots of molasses and pickles in five and ten-gallon kegs. When they got vegetables, they got them in large

lots and buried them in what were called root-houses. These were dug underground, except for the roof, which was like a mound just at ground level. It was cool and dark in the root-houses, and vegetables would keep a long time."

"I see you brought your guitar" is what Smokey said as Billy Shortstack approached his porch and took the guitar off her back."

"If Mama doesn't need to make a loaf of bread we've got a little time. Let's try that Darkness tune again."

Smokey filled his jelly jar with his latest batch of blackberry wine and passed the jug along.

Then Smokey began to draw the bow across the fiddle, while Billy Shortstack and Katy Gunn joined in. Then those of us that knew the words began to sing.

In my hour of darkness
In my time of need
Oh, Lord grant me vision
Oh, Lord grant me speed

The there was an old man kind and wise with age
And he read me just like a book never missed a page
And loved him like a father,
And I loved him like my friend
And I knew his time could shortly come
But I did not know just when

Oh Lord, grant me vision oh, Lord grant me speed
Oh Lord, grant me vision oh, Lord grant me speed

Emmylou Harris & Gram Parsons (1972)

163

After all, it was Sunday Night Bible Study Class.

This from an interview conducted by William C. Haight with a lady named Mrs. Ernest P. Truesdell, for the Federal Writer's Project. (1939)

"At a series of meetings, we had a tall, stately, dynamic, southern revivalist leading the congregation into less sinful paths. His silver tongue could tell the saloon element they were heading for Hell in more ways than you would think possible. The women would hear the tales of Hell-fire and pack them home and unload on their less active religious husbands. It was a standing joke that everybody stayed up an hour later during the nights the revivalist was in town, so the wives could rail at their husbands."

The Swimming Hole

During the summer months, when the July sun started making that little part of the world July hot, those clear, snow fed, mountain streams began to beckon. A Siren's song, it was. They invited us in for a swim after the Day Shift ended, or before the Swing Shift began, or even in the mornings after that Graveyard Shift was done.

Those high mountain streams invited us in to clear the mind of muddy thoughts before peaceful, cool, clear, well-earned, sleep.

It was only natural I suppose. The sun was there. So was sparkling, cool, mountain water running over thoughtful dabbling feet. So was deep green summer grass and willow; pine and cattail; and a cool deep pool with summer salmon lying peaceful and quite where the ripple stilled.

Muscle and strong backs built a diving board out a piece of sixteen inch wide lagging fastened to the bank with granite boulders as big as could be rolled; lagging that Timothy O'Leary had liberated from the Cougar Decline's timber storage shed and tossed into the back of his pickup truck on the twentieth day of July, 1978.

One had to be careful with one's bouncing on that diving board, however. Too much exuberant bouncing and the smooth, round, granite stones that fastened that diving board to the bank would roll out of the way, letting that diving board, along with whoever was doing the bouncing, to tumble into the shallow rocky bottom of that creek next to the bank.

It is somewhat remarkable in many ways how young people found that place, to my way of thinking. A swimming hole in an icy cold mountain stream and there they are.

There were those that had come looking for work, those of us who had found work, and those probably just passing through.

Opportunity had arisen and some of us had found a niche and a payday, mostly because we had gotten to that niche first.

The boss said we were miners, and I guess that is exactly what we were.

A big piece of life for us was rock, dirt, black mud, and as hard as you could go until the end of the shift. That's just the way it was. When a shift was over there was an indisputable need to seek a cleansing inundation to remove the mud and muck that had found its way into the crevasses and pours in our skin. A token, end of the day ablution, before crawling between clean sheets just wouldn't do.

If you were young, so inclined, and didn't feel like waiting on the shower down at Dog Patch to warm you could wash that dirt off in a clean, swift moving mountain stream. Get out of hole, hang your diggers and your cloths in that old willow tree, take a deep breath, brace yourself for the cold, and leap. Mother Nature and that swift moving stream would take it all away in an instant; the mud riveling down your back, the grunge around your eyes and the uncertainties that might have clouded your mind.

Freedoms just another word for nothing left to lose
Nothing ain't worth nothing, but it's free.

166

Feeling good was easy lord
When she sang the blues
Feeling good was good enough for me
Good enough for me, and Bobby McGee.

Kris Kristofferson (1970)

I think we were all endowed with bodies and bones made of elastic and rubber; inured to the cold of those snow fed mountain streams.

Then there was Katy Gunn, over the twenties, but not by much. She was thirty-two when she timidly tested that water with the tip of her big toe. She was also anything but free of a troubled mind.

It was Timothy O'Leary that pushed her off the end of that diving board. At first Katy thought she should be angry, but she wasn't. She was wet, cold, and exhilarated. There wasn't much of anything else for Katy to consider right then. Life for her, at that moment, was just that simple; wet, cold... and exhilarated.

Timothy O'Leary: "I told you that if you came to the swimming hole with me you'd forget about that letter you got from your son."

"Are you nuts?" As Katy Gunn wiped the water out of her eyes.

"Now you're one of us." as Timothy O'Leary pulled his knees up against his chest and created a roaring splashed in the water right beside her

"One of what?" was Katy's quite logical question.

Alice was there, with new friend named Billy Shortstack that she had come to know up at the Store during that first cold winter and that first early spring; sitting on the grassy bank in cut off blue jeans and tank tops, water dripping from their hair down the creases in their backs; laughing.

I don't suppose that creek ran as clear back when the mines up-creek from that swimming hole were operational in the early part of the twentieth century.

Back then they dumped their tailings and effluent from their portals directly into the stream. It wasn't even considered a sin back then, that's just the way things were done. The water probably ran muddy and turbid until the sediment settled, then tinted red from oxides in the ore bodies.

If you were to look on the other side of that swimming hole, in the summer of 1978, you might have seen a yellow flower growing near some loosely piled rocks that may have been a fence at one time.

That flower is not a native. It was a Cornflower from a different place and time, when a different Katy planted it to remind her of a home far away. Katrina's sister put a hand full of seeds in a small pouch that she had sewn from worn sacking in the bottom of her brother's haversack before he left the little coastal town in what used to be Prussia for the Atlantic coast of the United States in 1902. Vasily arrived in Granite, Oregon, leading ten head of mule belonging to a man named Charles Dabney out of Ketchum Idaho, in 1904.

According the 1880 census sixty four percent of the population of Granite proper were Chinese from Kwangtung Province.

From Miss Neil Nevin: A citizen of Granite in the late 1800s

168

"When Granite was at its height there were approximately 3000 Chinese working in the mines, or working mines of their own. These Chinese would buy mines after the white man was nearly finished with his operations. Usually the white man was convinced of the fact that he was selling slag dirt. However, the Chinese could still make a living from the tailings or slags. This always struck me as a peculiar but profitable quality."

"The poor Chinese were socially ostracized from white society. However, they had their own lives and led them much as we do ours. They even practiced their oriental religions".

"Occasionally some one of the whites would brave the criticism of the occidentals and attend the Chinese services."

"Respectable business houses in Granite made it a point of pride in not hiring any Chinese labor. This seems cruel today but perhaps the situation justified it. You see, the Mongolians greatly outnumbered the whites."

Timothy O'Leary
Jugando Con Oro

"Where did you find this?"

That was Timothy O'Leary commenting on a black, crumbly, rough shaped bit of rock sitting in the palm of his hand. A rock stitched throughout with wire-like strands of gold.

"By that big culvert down on Cracker Creek, just below where all the little Cracker Creeks run together. Laying there in the backfill. It probably got dumped in there when the county got that culvert put back together after it washed out during the runoff this spring. I also found quite a few iron laced chunks of quartz lying around in the same place." That was Jim's reply.

Jim's obvious intention was to entice Timothy O'Leary's curiosity.

The first time I ever saw Jim he was up to his knees in Clear Creek, just before Thanksgiving Day in the year 1977. He was trying to collect the iron pyrite floating down the stream with a soup spoon and a rusty old coffee pot he probably found lying around in front of an old mine adit somewhere in that part of the world. I guess Jim didn't know that although pyrite was gold in color it still wasn't the gold he was looking for. He wasn't even enlightened to the fact that the gold he sought was a weighty mineral and not very likely to be floating down an ice-cold creek in the month of November in the first place.

In the summer of 1978, Jim and Alice were living in a little camp trailer in the North Fork campground that Thor had sold them for little down, adjustable payments, and little profit. Thor had offered that little wheeled abode after he found them huddled together in a heavy old sleeping bag in the back of an old Studebaker station wagon down near McCully Forks.

Life for Jim and Alice was a whole lot improved over that life's very beginnings on the west side of the Elkhorn Ridge; the beginnings of a life they wouldn't have even considered if they were a few years older and a little less naïve about what those mountains in the eastern part of Oregon had to offer.

It was an old-timer by the name of George Spears that heard of Jim and Alice's plight, via Thor, that had shown Jim what gold was and how to pan for it.

Jim would clamber over the boulders and push his way through the brush along the sides of the many side streams with a shovel and a gold pan. He would find a likely spot, wash a little sand and gravel, and every so often he would find a little gold. He'd take a wooden matchstick, stick that little piece of gold residing in the bottom of that pan to the end of that matchstick, and then he would tap that little piece of gold off the end of that matchstick into a one-ounce vial that he carried in his button-down shirt pocket.

By the end of the summer of 1978 Jim was working at the Cougar and prospecting for gold in the time he had to spare. He was gold miner in every since of the word; for richer; for poorer; and all points in between.

.

This from an interview conducted by William C. Haight with a lady he referred to only as "Mrs. Brown," a citizen of Canyon City Oregon, in approximately 1868.

"Father worked for the Wells Fargo Company and had the stage line from The Dalles to Canyon City.

Every Saturday morning the Chinese would line up outside of my father's business with their bags of gold dust to be weighed and shipped to San Francisco. I can still hear the clock-clock-clock of the Chinese as they talked to my father. They seemed to like him quite well. Often, father would have me come over to the office and sew the canvas he had into bags to hold the gold dust."

"The Chinese were an honest, industrious race of people. Most everyone in Canyon City had at least one working for him. Too, the poor fellows were often the source of much amusement and the butt of many a practical joke in this rough and ready mining camp."

"The mining they did was quite different than the white man's. Usually, the Chinese washed the gravel which the white man had thrown out as waste. They made a good deal of money by using the tailings left by the whites."

"Alambre de oro, y una muy buena pieza, lo es." said Timothy O'Leary as he rolled that piece of rock around in the palm of his hand

"Do you ever wonder what the actual value of gold is?" That was a question Timothy O'Leary asked Jim. He and Jim were sitting on the workbench in the Dry while the smoke from the last round cleared.

"A hundred twenty-seven dollars and twenty-seven cents per ounce... troy." Was Jim's robust reply.

"If you took all the gold used to make jewelry, what would be leftover?" Timothy O'Leary was about to have one of life's little epiphanies. "Those pocket calculators have gold plated contacts, I guess. How much gold is left after all its practical applications take their piece... and where does it go?"

Jim was cleverly getting involved in one of Timothy O'Leary's little epiphanies. "They can roll it out into real thin sheets. A little of it can go a long ways" as he was getting a nugget the size of a small pea out of the vial in his lunch bucket.

"El oro es atesorado porque es oro." was Timothy O'Leary's answer to his own question as to where the extra gold went.

"Y eso es un poco más de oro!" Is what Timothy O'Leary said when he saw that little nugget in Jim's hand. "Oro!"

Timothy O'Leary had never seen gold in its native state before. However, Timothy was a geologist working in a gold mine, and Jim figured to get Timothy involved in helping him find the vein from where that piece of wire gold came.

Timothy O'Leary's first schooling in gold mining ended in Ecuador with a three-hundred- and-fifty-dollar check written on an American bank. Then, in 1978, he was starting to get an idea of how things worked in and around Granite, Oregon.

Party at the Store

*I*t was a hot summer's day, that first summer, that first year, 1978.

Someone – it may have been Lance; maybe not – took it upon themselves to stretch a volleyball net across Main Street in front of the Granite Store. Whoever that someone was tied that net to the post that supported the porch roof next to those steps, making it nearly impossible to come and go from the Store without passing into the volleyball court and into the volleyball game that eventually ensued.

Whoever that someone was also added a lot of noise and dust to the air.

Those volleyball games – or perhaps a better explanation would have been the 'Organized Chaos' spinning around a shabby white ball – got quite intense at times, with a cast of characters entering and exiting the game at will; diving in the dirt; scooping in the gravel; road rash; bumping heads; that sort of thing. Sandals and cut off blue jeans, cowboy boots, logging boots, moccasins, bare-chested, torn shirts, laughing, yelling, cussing, and sweat; all mixed together in a jumble in the middle of the volleyball court.

"This toe is broken, I'm pretty sure... I don't know about this one."

"Put this cotton up your nose and put your head back. It'll stop bleeding pretty soon."

A person from conventional society would have been amazed at the kind of people showing up at

174

the parties that Lance sponsored. Every nonconventional social stripe found representation there. A person would have had to wonder where they came from and how they got there.

Some came with a guitar, or a fiddle, maybe a banjo... and a tune.

Then those fiddles and guitars might form a band, or a band already formed would appear, pick up the beat, and the volleyball court would become a dancing ground.

Then Sonny would bring out a clear liquid in a gallon jug – a moonshine made in Virginia by very skilled hands – that he would share with all so inclined.

Sonny had a daughter, about fifteen years of age, that had learned the guitar, and Sonny liked to have her heard.

Billy Shortstack would begin to play, and sing.

Livin' in the city
Ain't never been my idea of gettin' it on
But the job demands that you make new plans
Before your big chance is gone
You get a house in the hills
You're payin' everyone's bills
And they tell you that you're gonna go far
But in the back of my mind
I hear it time after time
"Is that who you really are?"

The crowd would like what they heard and then applaud, then that impromptu band would pick up the beat, just a little more.

"Talkin' on the telephone
Settin'up another day of people to meet
You've gotta do what's right
You've gotta spend the night
Stayin' in touch with the street
When you're surrounded by friends
They say the fun never ends
But I guess I'll never figure it out
'Cause in the back of my mind I
hear it time after time
"Is this what it's all about?"

Johnny R Cash (1972)

Sonny's people, those folks from the Blue Ridge Mountains in Virginia, knew how to clog, they did. Men in denim, plaid cotton shirts, and heavy boots. Women, barefooted, in light cotton dresses covered with faded red flowers. Their children; swinging and being swung. The music setting the rhythm – or maybe it was those boots setting the beat, it's hard to say – on that hard-wooden floor.

The porch of the Granite Store would become a venue for clogging and the volleyball court became a tribal dance with dust in the air.

In the cool of the evening… that first summer… of the year 1978.

This from Joe Strangle. Taken from an interview conducted by William Haight for the Federal Writers Project (1939)

"God, I allus was a fool for dances. We sure did hoe down in them square dances. That's where I learnt to clog

so good. No girl would have nothin' to do with you unless you could ho'er down and clog."

"I was one of the best cloggers around there. I reckon this was because I weren't Irish. All of them Irish feller's would dance one or two dances, then go out and fight. I allus danced."

"We would dance some round dances too."

"First four right and left
Second four left and right
Hi HO Katy
The Irish Queen"

It Could Happen

"It is an experience common to all men to find that, on any special occasion, such as the production of a magical effect for the first time in public, everything that can go wrong will go wrong. Whether we must attribute this to the malignity of matter or to the total depravity of inanimate things, whether the exciting cause is hurry, worry, or what not, the fact remains."

Nevil Maskelyne (1908)

Simplistically Stated: "Whatever can go wrong will go wrong."

It didn't take all that long for us to get that one figured out. That little axiom eventually became "Rule Number One."

Take a new miner, and he/she is going to have to make the requisite number of mistakes every new miner is going to make. Maybe not all at once. Maybe not all reserved for new miners, but mistakes are going to be made. That is just the way things are. It is not written down a on paper anywhere that I know of. Call it a relatively dependable theory, maybe even a fact.

"It can happen with a rattle, hump, and a bang."

We had gotten back from a weekend down in Baker City and things were just a little messed up; not the way we wanted to start the week: Katy Gunn, Timothy O'Leary, Jim, and I. Not totally abnormal for that place. The pumps in the Decline would plug, blow a discharge hose, blow a fuse, or just shut down if they felt like it. Not an everyday occurrence, but it would happen.

The pump in number one sump had caught a rock and jammed tight. Muddy water overflowed that sump and ran back down the Decline to sump number two. That gave number two the water it got from the Face and the water it had already pumped up to number one. Then the Face pump gave up, leaving a rutted washed-out road and a Face under twenty feet of mucky water.

There was not much to be done; rebuild the road, pump the Face out, dig the drills out of the muck, and get back to it.

A four hundred sixty-volt submersible pump was placed in the bucket of the mucker, then that mucker drove out in the water a ways. When that water was pumped out of the way, the mucker would be moved out into the water a little more.

Katy Gunn was running that mucker, or rather sitting in it reading a book called "At Play in the Fields of the Lord" that she had picked up off Timothy O'Leary's chair next to that gloriously warm pot-bellied stove in Dog Patch on that cold fifth of December morning.

Katy would ease the front wheels of that mucker down that fifteen percent grade decline into the water until the pump stopped gurgling, set the parking brake, fish Timothy's wet and getting wetter book out of her diggers, adjust her light so that the pages weren't too harshly lit, and resume her reading. When the pump in the mucker bucket broke suction and began slurping and gurgling

179

again, she would move the mucker forward a little bit more.

The lift lever on that mucker had developed a hydraulic leak. It would slowly raise the boom while sitting at an idle, just a little at a time. Katy knew the boom would rise. She would reach out with her left hand every so often and give that lift lever a gentle tap forward, and the boom would settle back down.

I guess you could say Katy got a little involved in that book she was reading, or she dozed off wishing she was in that warm South American jungle that Timothy O'Leary was always talking about in his, quite often, annoying Spanish lingo.

I'm sure that Katy would much rather have been anywhere other than strapped into a not so comfortable seat in the dripping wet, cold, and dark, listening to the whine of that pump and the idle of that mucker.

The boom on that mucker lifted all the way to the back – and Kay Gunn did not notice. Then the bucket on the end of that boom scissored a four-inch airline in two. The blast of air that followed was supersonic at the very least. The air around us filled with water vapor as the hundred and forty pounds of air pressure fought its way out of the confinement of that pipe with a screaming roar so loud Jim, Timothy, and I had to squeeze our hands over our ears.

This is where Katy Gunn made the second half of her mistake. I'll bet she didn't set the emergency brake. I'll bet she just had her foot on the brake peddle, and the air pressure that ran those brakes bled off. I'll bet she slapped the boom lever all the way forward when she awoke to the fact that it was the bucket on the piece of equipment she was driving that had caused such total unfathomable chaos, and I'll wager that when that bucket came down out of the timber that held the back up that mucker took off to the deep and black; under twenty feet of muddy, cold, water.

What I saw by the beam of my light as Katy went by, on her way down and under, through the churning vapor, noise and confusion, was a clenched jaw and wide staring eyes wondering what to do.

"Pull the emergency brake!... Step on the brake!... Get off of that thing!... Jump!"

Katy went under that water, along with that mucker... and that four hundred sixty-volt submersible pump. A pump which severed its power cable as soon as that cable got to short. A severed power cable that produced a blinding arc of white light as the high voltage electricity of that cable tried to find a place to ground, adding to the confusion all round.

Jim didn't exactly know what to do, but he knew he had to do something. He had gathered his senses enough by then to get a semblance of what was going on into his mind. He crouched low near the power box and shut the electricity off that used to go to that pump, ending that blinding white light, giving us one less vector to factor into the equation.

It was Timothy O'Leary that got Katy out of that mucker's seat.

He stepped out of his diggers, boots and utility belt in no more than three quick moves and was in the water headed for those submerged taillights and

181

bubbles coming from that mucker's flooded engine before there was time to say "Jack Straw."

Even if she didn't have time to suck in a good lung of air before she went under Katy prob- ably maintained enough presence of mind to reach down and unbuckle her seatbelt before Timothy reached down into that dark mass of freezing confusion and grabbed her by the jacket of her diggers and dragged her out.

It was I that figured out what went on with the air, and dashed the hundred yards back up the Decline to the valve header and shut that air off.

When I got back to where it began all was fairly silent. Other than the ringing in my ears and little hiss of compressed air through a leaky valve there wasn't much to hear.

Jim was standing there, shining his light on Katy Gunn and Timothy O'Leary who were sitting on the berm next to the rib, the water draining out of their clothes rippling down the Decline to the flooded Face. Timothy sitting with his arms on his knees, staring down between his feet while Katy was pulling off a boot and emptying the cold water out.

Katy Gunn had that book of Timothy O'Leary's sitting beside her in the rocks. She handed it back to Timothy after she put her boot on.

Timothy O'Leary squeezed the pages between his shaking hands; gauging that books condition by the amount of water draining out.

"How far did you get?"

"Page one hundred and twenty-six," was Katy's reply.

Then Timothy O'Leary began to sing; a nervous, grateful way of signing, as he pulled his boots on, put his hard hat back on his head, strapped on his belt and battery pack and adjusted the beam of his light... as he grabbed Katy's hand and started leading her up that decline toward the cold winter air and the bright winter daylight.

I'm goin' up the country, baby don't you want to go?
I'm goin' up the country, baby don't you want to go?
I'm goin' to some place, I've never been before
I'm goin' I'm goin' where the water tastes like wine
I'm goin' where the water tastes like wine
We can jump in the water, stay drunk all the time

I'm gonna leave this city, got to get away
I'm gonna leave this city, got to get away
All this fussin' and fightin' man, you know
I sure can't stay
So baby pack your leavin'
You know we've got to leave today
Just exactly where we're goin'
I cannot say
But we might even leave the U.S.A.
It's a brand-new game, that I want to play

Alan Wilson (1968)

Timothy O'Leary's logbook entry that night was short, but quite profound.

"There are very definitely those blunders that are going to sneak up from behind and bite you on the ass when you're not looking."

Timothy O'Leary (December 5th, 1978)

183

It Was Sunday Night

It was not more than a week after Katy Gunn had driven that mucker underwater and almost drowned. It was nearly Christmas, the twelfth of December 1978, a Sunday night, and Reverend Paulson came around.

We were told not to accustom ourselves to the Reverend's appearance during the deep snow winter months, for the road beyond Dog Patch was not plowed of snow, and there was plenty of it. Snow chest high to a tall man in most places.

But this Sunday was a little different and Reverend arrived totally unexpected via the North Fork Highway through Sumpter. I would suppose that the Reverend's intention was to pay those of us in that part of the world a special visit at the expense of his other congregations residing on the other side of those drifted snows.

We usually had Sunday Night Bible Study Class outside on that large veranda hooked to the front of Smokey and Angelina's cozy little place during the spring, summer and early fall of the year, as the sun began to melt into the horizon and the Milky Way and its brethren stars began to make appearance through the tops of those tall Pines all around. But this was the winter of the year, and the Reverend Paulson a total surprise, so Sunday Night Bible Study Class was held next to that big pot-bellied wood-burning stove, in that big two-story building, in that place we called Dog Patch.

Angelina's meal that night was no more than canned stew and buttered Wonder Bread prepared by her and Timothy O'Leary on the propane camp stove in the kitchen.

Smokey poured each of us his finest raspberry wine that night. He poured it into our finest crystal he did; tin cups and jelly jars.

Smokey's flagon started out being a little prickly and stickery on top, then a little more urbane and wine-like about halfway down, then quite ample and countrified towards the bottom. It was there, on the very bottom of that gallon jug, a layer of syrup, so thick a mere sip would make a meal, awaited the last sojourner to hold forth his cup for a refill.

"Deal the cards, Reverend." That was Cecil.

"I am among you as the one who serves." said the Reverend as he started dealing a hand of Seven Card Stud. "The kings of the Gentiles exercise lordship over them, and those in authority over them are called benefactors – Two of spades."

"I hear you had a near calamity out here a few days ago?" The Reverend was looking at Katy Gunn when he asked that question and laid the last card down – And the three of diamonds."

"Oh, and I did." Said Katy Gunn trying on the Reverend's mischievous tone of voice. "And how is it you know of this near calamity."

"Isn't it amazing how word gets around," as the Reverend dealt Cecil his last card." Your wager" while looking at Katy Gunn.

"I'm in." As Katy Gunn's quarter landed on the brown plaid blanket draped over that big wooden cable spool, followed by four more shiny quarters – quarters leftover from bets laid on the shuffleboard table at Cattle Kate's the night before.

185

Then a Half-Dollar.

Angelina: "I'll raise a quarter."

"I only got dollars... Got any extra quarters.

Sunday Night Bible Study Class, for us at any rate, was not very strict on formality, but it was the Sunday Night Bible Study Class. The Reverend saw to that. And sometimes he made it a little personal.

The Reverend: "Did you think about the fact that you might die?"

Katy Gunn: "Not much... I was a little busy."

"Did you talk to the Lord while you were busy?"

"I don't think so." Katy said, thumbing up the ends of those cards up in front of her and having a precursory look for an Ace of Diamonds... her voice starting to get a little testy.

"I did." That was Timothy O'Leary. "Heard myself talking to him the whole time... I kept thinking: God damn! God damn! God damn!"

The Reverend: "We all talk to God when you stop to think about it, don't we? I mean you might not get down on your knees, but you do, in one way or another. Even when you might need to be getting out of the way. I'll bet you're talking to your God the whole time. We all do... Don't we?"

"Oh Jesus, let me win those nickels." That was Cecil – two threes and the One-Eyed Jack showing under his hand.

Smokey: "I fold."

Katy Gunn: "I'm done."

"Me too" throwing my cards into the center of that makeshift table.

Timothy O'Leary: "That's the end of it for me."

Angelina: "I'm folding, also."

The Reverend: "And when he came to take his spoils, he found much among them: goods, garments, and valuable things which he took for himself, more than he could carry."

"Deal em again Reverend. I like what you do" as Cecil raked in his plunder.

Angelina: "I talk to God. Nearly every time he starts shift," looking stiffly at Smokey. "He's getting to old for that kind of work.... and I also said "Thank you Lord" when you guys brought Katy down and got her in that hot shower. And I'll say it again... Thank You Lord!" As she took Cecil's jelly jar and set it off to the side a little bit, letting Cecil know that she had her eye on him. Letting Cecil know it was Sunday Night Bible Study Class and not entirely a game of Seven Card Stud.

Smokey began to slide the bow across his fiddle and hum a little tune... just to devil Angelina a bit, with that easy smile he always carried on his face when occasion called for it.

I can't stay here much longer, Melinda
The sun is getting high
I can't help you with your troubles
If you won't help with mine
I gotta get down I gotta get down
Gotta get down to the mine

You keep me up just one more night I can't stop here
no more
Big Ben clock says quarter to eight

187

You kept me up till four
I gotta get down I gotta get down
Or I can't work there no more

Can I go, buddy, can I go down Take your shift at the
mine
Gotta get down to the Cumberland mine
Gotta get down to the Cumberland mine
That's where I mainly spend my time

Make good money, five dollars a day
If I made any more, I might move away

Jerry Garcia (1970)

This from an interview conducted by William C.
Haight with the Reverend W.C. Driver for the Federal
Writer's Project. (1939)

"In the southern part of the state there were children
as old as 20 that had never heard a Christian service. They
would walk miles to hear the preacher in the railway car.
The novelty of the car probably attracted them as much as
the religious side. Children generally were delighted with
the idea of going to church in a railway car." (1895)

Television

I don't think television, least ways for my associates and I, made an appearance in Granite until that second winter. I'm quite sure that television had been tried in the past, seeing as how television in most civilized circles had become a necessity, but Granite, situated where it was, and what it was, hadn't been blessed with full reception… just yet.

I don't recollect seeing a television antenna sitting on the Marshal's home, nor Thor's, nor anyone's, for that matter.

By the time that second winter rolled in and over the top of us, Victor, Marlene, and Little Lola's position had improved a tolerable amount. They no longer lived in that little camp trailer next to those rickety stairs that lead up to that shower room door at Dog Patch. They now lived in one of those ramshackle houses that sat on the Cougar Mine property; a dwelling that probably was home to a 1920s hard rock miner and his family.

Many improvements had been made at the Cougar since my arrival that first winter. A lot of progress since George had stumped onto the scene and become the "Boss," as he let it be known.

Trenches from a natural spring up by the First Level were dug and pipes lain for indoor running water to Sonny's, Thor's, and Victor's place. Then Kitchen sinks were set into counters nailed to the walls, and hot water heaters were grafted on to provide hot water for dishes, showers and baths.

189

Victor and Sonny had refurbished Victor's "new" old house over the spring and summer of that year – 1978 – and it had become a fairly comfortable dwelling for Victor, Marlene, and red headed, bandy legged, Little Lola, who was now three years old. Victor and Marlene's bed was located in the same room as Little Lola's, along with the kitchen, and the dining room.

The only separate room in that house was a shed roofed building tacked onto the side as part of Sonny and Victor's initial refurbishment. When that bathroom was first completed Marlene and Little Lola had to walk to the outside door to get in, but as the winters snows deepened, and the need arose, a door size opening was cut in the wall near the foot of Little Lola's bed and hung over with a heavy wool blanket for entrance to that newly installed toilet and shower.

George's residence was palatial compared to others in and around. For one thing it wasn't put together somewhere between the 1920s and the 1930s. George's abode was sitting on a concrete foundation and built of freshly cut pine, red fir and Western Larch – lumber cut on the same mill Sonny used to cut the mines timber – and there were four rooms instead of two. After all, George was the boss.

Victor found it in that second hand store down there in Baker City, and I don't know if he even considered the fact that there might be a reason there were no televisions in Granite at that time.

He set that TV in the corner away from the stove that kept the place warm and fiddled the rabbit ears

190

around, too little, or no, effect. He then added a length of coat hanger, and some aluminum foil, also too little effect. He then stuck an aluminum pop can on top of all that, and he thought he saw a little movement, perhaps a Saturday morning Scooby Doo cartoon in the year 1978.

On another trip to the second hand store, down there in Baker City, he bought a sophisticated antenna at a bargain price, grafted that antenna to an old broom handle, stuck that broom handle in the outside snow, and a picture could be seen. That fact, in and of itself, helped turn Victor, Marlene, and Little Lola's, little abode into a gathering place on many a cold winter night in the month January, 1979.

It was Super Bowl XIII.

It was also the month of January, the deepest snows of the year, and the best reception on Victor's TV

We gathered there, Cecil, Timothy O'Leary and I – in front of Victor's TV – served popcorn, chips, and beer, by Little Lola and Marlene, who could have cared less about the highly hyped football game that was about to be presented on that television. Company for them was a rarity and always welcome, no matter the circumstances.

"We need to move the antenna," was Victor's instruction. That "We" – meaning me – for you see, it was I that plowed the snow out of the road in front of Victor's house and had accidentally tilted that antenna a bit off angle, worsening that televisions reception in the eyes of the beholders gathered round.

"Turn it a little to the left... no the other left," was Victor's instruction, yelled out the window. "There... I can see Tom Landry ... No, there he goes... move the antenna down the road a little bit. Over there... out away from that big pine... There."

It was then the clouds began to part, letting the UHF signal escape to the stratosphere instead of bouncing off the clouds and coming down to Victor's TV. Before the first quarter was over the fuzzy picture on that TV had become unintelligible for those hunkered forwards with anticipation.

"It's a fumble! who's got the ball?"

"We've got to move that antenna again." That "We" ... meaning me, of course.

I had just about gotten my hands on the antenna when the clouds finished drifting together again allowing the television signal from Spokane, or Boise, or maybe it was Portland, to bounce down and reach that antenna, blessing all in front of Victor's TV a fairly decent black and fuzzy white view.

"There." Was Victor's voice out that window on the east side of he, Marlene's, and little Lola's house.

"Where's he at?" Was Victor's question. "He's over there." Was Cecil's reply, pointing to me over by the stove.

And so it went. Eventually we all took a turn moving and adjusting that antenna to improve reception, with exception of Victor, Marlene, and Little Lola, of course. After all, it was their television.

By the fourth quarter our knowledge of that football game was about the same as the reception on that TV; all broken up into little fuzzy pieces; the yelling of the crowd; barley intelligible players scampering around on the field. The terse commentary of Curt Gowdy above it all.

"What just happened?"

"The NFL championship belongs to ...."Fuzz, static ...

"Who won?...Who won?"

It was Victor, sitting in front of that TV, on Little Lola's very short stool, with his arms between his knees, fiddling with the vertical hold, a pouty, frustrated, expression on his face that caused Marlene to offer up a bit of a giggle. That little giggle, of course, gave Timothy O'Leary incentive to cop a bit of a giggle. Then all of us had to give a hearty laugh.

Little Lola was standing next to Victor with her hand on his shoulder, waiting on her daddy.

It was then Victor's angst turned to a little grin, and the evening ended on a fine and final note, as we all high fived one another and walked out the door, towards our warm beds, on that cold winter's night.

When I drove through Granite in 1982, I saw that a few of those new satellite dishes had made an appearance; those first satellite dishes that were ten feet diameter; looking like they would be for military application rather than television reception. I wondered what the reception was like at the time. I wondered then how many channels were available.

193

It's my understand that a person with the latest technology can get as many as three hundred channels these days, and could probably thumb up any Superbowl, day of the week, if they so chose.

Guns

Today I heard the cold winds moanin' and I saw some
geese up on the wings
A southern home waits their returnin' oh that'd be
such a lucky thing
Nobody cares where I am goin' and I don't remember
where I've been
I only know the cold winds blowin' and winter's
comin' on again
Once I was young and had a reason for doing
everything I did
A pretty girl for every season without a conscience to
forbid
And I used to know someone in this town someone I
used to call a friend
But we ain't walkin' on the same ground and
winter's comin' on again

Dick Curless (1972)

There was a Halloween party at the Store, and some of the folks that lived out and around were quite enthusiastic about the event.

A few people went as mountain men, which wasn't all that far from what they actually were; just a little more contemporary. One gentleman came in buckskin leggings and a loin cloth and spent most of that night next to the stove trying to keep his butt warm.

Timothy O'Leary went as a Mississippi Gambler with an unloaded forty four pistol under his Mississippi River Gamblers costume.

I don't know where Timothy got that Mississippi River Gamblers ensemble. I know there weren't many costume shops in that part of the world at that time. That costume was very ornate one, and that's a fact: a long swallow-tailed coat, ruffled cravat, ruffled cuffs with ruby cufflinks, and a broad brimmed Mississippi River gamblers hat.

I witnessed Timothy O'Leary pull that pistol he had secreted in that Mississippi Gambler's Suit on the Marshal. All in good fun to Timothy O'Leary's way of thinking... not so to the Marshal.

"What in the hell are you doing?"

"Gotcha, didn't I?" Was Timothy O'Leary's reply.

Bud and Timothy knew each other well enough. Bud knew Timothy, and he knew that this was the often-impulsive Timothy O'Leary's idea of a funny prank, but it still didn't sit very well with him. I would suppose Marshal Bud thought it was a little more than rude to pull a for-real pistol, even if unloaded, on someone, no matter how well you knew that person.

There were those who wanted to carry pistols in the Granite Store back then. A few camped down by those old placer workings on Granite, Bull Run and Clear Water Creeks mostly. Not many, but some. I think they were into playing cowboy more than anything else: Colt 45 revolvers displayed in leather side holsters strapped on the hip in the quick draw fashion like those portrayed in western movies of the time.

Bud had worn a pistol of that style ever since I'd known him. After all, he was the Marshal. I guess you could say it was part of his persona; that pistol, his Stetson hat, and that tin star.

Guns were there and I doubt anybody even thought about it very much, but that business with Timothy O'Leary put a different perspective on things as far as the Marshal's thinking went, and he wanted not to have pistols in the store anymore.

I don't think anyone would say Marshal Bud was exactly taciturn. He usually said what was needed and plenty extra if he felt it necessary, and this was one of those times.

He just put the word out. He more or less told all of us through the grape vine that he didn't think beer, guns, and Timothy O'Leary belonged in the same place at the same time.

The Marshal's wishes were respected for the most part. After all, he was the Marshal. The pistols found themselves under the driver's seat, or hanging at whatever was called home on a peg by the stove.

But there was going to be one exception, and that one exception was going to be Harley. Everyone knew it. Especially Marshal Bud. Bud figured he was going to have to argue and cajole, and he didn't want to, especially with the likes of Harley.

A few days later Harley arrived, as expected. He had indeed heard the Marshal's request, and he was indeed carrying a pistol on his hip, as expected. He'd come for no better reason than to test the Marshal's resolve.

When he mounted the steps to the Store Marshal Bud was waiting, leaning on the porch post next to the stairs.

"Harley, why do you figure you need to wear that damned thing in here?"

Harley got a little smile on his face about that time. Then he just unstrapped his pistol, handed it to the Marshal, and walked on into the store without a word. That was it…. with exception of the fact that Bud was standing on the front porch of the Granite Store with Harleys pistol in his hand and he didn't quite know what to do with it.

(That was probably Harley's act of defiance and his acquiescence to the need for some sort of civil authority all rolled into one.)

And now Bud, being that civil authority, had acquired Harley's pistol and felt he had also acquired responsibility for its care.

When I pulled up in front of the Store there sat the Marshal in that old rocking chair, wrapped in a heavy winter coat, sitting under that bare light bulb, reading a book, and there was a pistol in a holster that wasn't his setting on the end table next to him.

Bud had picked up one of those Reader's Digest Condensed Books from that bookcase setting next to Willie's Jukebox. I think it was "At Play in the Fields of the Lord" that the Marshal was reading when Harley came out about an hour later.

"Sorry I was out of line there Bud." Harley said that with a sly grin on his face while putting his thumbs into the belt loops of his pants.

Bud riffled through a few pages then popped that book shut with a sort of agitated look on his face. He thought about it for a little bit, then he gave a sigh and started thumbing back through the pages in his book again, back to page one hundred and twenty-six, so he wouldn't have to look at Harley and said, "Just about what I expected. Don't forget your pistol... and say hello to Dar for me."

A young cowboy named Billy Joe grew restless on the farm
A boy filled with wanderlust who really meant no harm
He changed his clothes and shined his boots
And combed his dark hair down
And his mother cried as he walked out

Don't take your guns to town son
Leave your guns at home Bill
Don't take your guns to town

Johnny R Cash (1958)

Bunny's Tale

According to the census taken in 1980 the population of Granite was seventeen – up from the 1970 census which was four – and there is a very good chance my name is on the census roles as a citizen of Granite at that time.

Bunny was the person who had taken the task of collecting the data, if you want to call it that, for the town of Granite and the surrounding vicinity - little dots on the map. Places like Willow, Greenhorn, Bates, Austin House, Olive, Bourne, Tipton... and all those little places hidden out in the trees and boulders in between.

"Census workers, or enumerators, gather data for the federal government. Their main job duties usually include interviewing citizens, validating residency, and gathering economic data for the U.S Census Bureau."
(Wikipedia)

A better job description might have been: "The person who is going to go out there, try and find whomever is out there, wherever they may be, and get their names, birthdays, and what they do, down on the appropriate lines on the appropriate forms."

Bunny and I were out at Cattle Kate's the night before. She was there in a pair of bib overalls over a fuzzy wool sweater, as if she was used to being out in the cold, and might be again, "So best be prepared."

Bunny wanted me to do her a favor. "Do you suppose you could take this poster up to the store and have Lance to put it up behind the bar?"

A poster with bold gold lettering emblazoned over a photograph of a pair of well-groomed hands in a business suit dropping a large envelope into one of those big blue mailboxes that used to set on every main street of every town with cement sidewalks in the USA.

"It is not too late to help your community get the funds it needs. It is not too late to answer the census. We are counting on you. Answer the census." That's what that poster said.

I doubt that census; that census taken in 1980. It seems to me that there were a lot more people than that around. There were those that lived in Granite proper, to be sure, and then there were those that didn't. There were those that lived in little cabins scattered throughout the trees and boulders of the surrounding countryside. Perhaps living in one of the few buildings left in a little mining town that did not exist anymore. A place like La Belleview, French Diggings, Austin, or Bourne.

The population of Granite in the year 1870 is said to be over four hundred. The 1880 census said that the population was around two hundred, nearly half the previous ten-year census.

This from Miss Neil Nevin. Eighteen years old, somewhere between those two census dates: 1870 and 1880.

201

"Working in the mines were a number of 'Cornish men'. These men were not a part of the group, really; but at times they would take part in the local entertainment. One time the Sunday school had them sing for us. They had beautiful voices, but they didn't know a note of music. One of the tenors entered a contest for the state fair and won first prize, using a guitar for accompaniment. Their cabins were off a ways from the rest of us and every evening you could hear them signing their songs, many of them original. Not being able to read and write they naturally found learning fairly hard. By making the music and words up they would fulfill their signing ambitions, although their songs were expressed in vile English."

Bunny had just gotten down onto what we used to call the North Fork Highway. She was walking back in the direction of Granite with that big leather briefcase in which she kept her census collecting accoutrements, along with a day's supply of sandwiches, canned fruit and pickles, slung over her shoulder when Thor pulled up beside her in his old Ford pickup.

"Are you broke down?"

"Back up that way about two miles," as she showed him a busted u-joint and a handful of greasy bearings in her right hand.

"Well, I guess I can see that, can't I?" Was Thor's reply.

Bunny did not know Thor personally. She knew him by reputation only. It was Lance that told her he was the man to see about getting that noisy u-joint fixed in that old car the Census Bureau gave her ten cents a mile to drive.

"Are you Thor?"

"Yea… that's me… That's Cabell City up there. Why you going up there?"

Bunny dropped that busted u-joint and those greasy bearings into Thor's outstretched hand. Then she pulled a form out of that briefcase with her greasy fingers. "I'm trying to find this guy."

"Harley? I know him. He and Dar live back up Greenhorn… About twenty miles the other direction."

"Well then who is that up there? There's a place that looks lived in, but I couldn't find any one around."

"That's Greener. He was probably watching you from the trees. He probably knows who you are and what you're doing by now. He don't trust the government."

"Well, that solves that one." As Bunny wrote "Greener" on the top line of the form with a leaky pen and greasy fingers. "I assume he's white and about thirty years old… right?"

"More like fifty."

Bunny writing in the proper space: "How long has he been a citizen of this locality."

"About two years."

Bunny, writing on the appropriate line and checking the appropriate box.

"Wife and kids?"

"Don't know… not here."

Writing on the appropriate line and checking the appropriate box.

Thor was on his way to do a little evening fishing up on the North Fork, but Bunny interested him.

It was then that he turned around and gave Bunny a ride back to Granite where he crawled under an old Chevy Impala that was sitting out in the trees behind what was left of that old drug store on Main Street and pulled the drive line.

Thor interested Bunny almost as much as Bunny interested Thor.

"Let's see. Thor?" As Bunny pulled another of those census forms out of that leather briefcase and got ready to fill in the appropriate lines and check off the appropriate boxes. "Is that your whole name, or is there more to it."

"Thüringen is the last name. My daddy was a Swede. A fisherman over on the coast back when I was a kid."

Hard Rock

The First Level. It's good rock. Rings sharp and clear – a little like the bell on that Big Ben alarm clock sitting on the floor next to the bed – when you'd tap the face with that two-pound hammer. Hard rock. Drill it, shoot it, muck it, bolt in a little mesh, and move on.

Clean cold air. In the mornings that air – scrubbed and polished from the mornings dew hanging on the grasses and the needles of Ponderosa Pine – would move up from the valley below and through the mined-out workings above. In the evenings, when the air outside began to cool, that air would turn around and go the opposite way, down through that mined out orebody and out the First Level's portal.

Twenty bucks a foot of advance. Two six- foot rounds per shift and extend service. That was thirty-six feet per day. Fifty cents a square foot of mesh, a buck a bolt. Seven dollars per foot of rail – and we got one hundred feet in one and a quarter shifts.

We'd hit it rich.

We'd been at it for a while, and we were getting good at it.

> *We dig, dig, dig, dig, dig, dig, dig in our mine the*
> *whole day through*
> *To dig, dig, dig, dig, dig, dig, dig is what we really*
> *like to do*
> *It ain't no trick to get rich quick*
> *If you dig dig dig with a shovel or a pick*
> *In a mine! In a mine! In a mine! In a mine!*

Where a million diamonds shine!
We dig, dig, dig, dig, dig, dig, dig from early morn
till night
We dig, dig, dig, dig, dig, dig, dig up everything in
sight
We dig up diamonds by the score
A thousand rubies, sometimes more
But we don't know what we dig 'em for We dig dig
dig a-dig dig

Frank Churchill & Larry Morey (1937) From Snow
White and the Seven Dwarfs

"All right you guys." With a doff of his hat to Katy Gunn. "I'll let you have it. But I'll be damned if I know how you got it. Man… that's drift driven." That was George handing out the checks on Friday night. "Big time at the Store tonight, and a bigger time at Cattle Kate's tomorrow, I'll bet."

We were young, and we were lean; filled with good food and an unworried, well earned, easy night's sleep. Red blood filled with Testosterone pumping through blue veins and purple arteries. The god of the day would quite probably been Mars.

"Get the drills up! We can beat that crew by four feet tonight if we hump it. Let's roll. The smokes almost clear!"

We'd argue, bend, cheat, and test one another. Then we mixed all that together. We had learned how to work together, we did. The cosmic tumblers were clicking into place, the planets were nearly in alignment, and we had our hands on something we could actually get hold of and understand: rock, powder, timber and sweat.

"Forget that! Grab that short piece of hose hidden in the. We'll drill the burn and leave that air line for them!"

We'd split forces, Jim and I. Jim was on the face and I was back up the drift a ways drilling the holes for a muck bay so that Katy Gunn could cut haulage time between rounds.

And there was this rock, you see; a Doney about the size of a beach ball hanging down from the Back. A hanging lump of loose rock stuck in the middle of solid rock all around, and I couldn't get that hump of rock barred loose. It ignored my every wish, my every desire; pry, poke and cuss as I might with the scaling bar… it would not move.

"It isn't going anywhere, is it?" That was Timothy O'Leary when he came down to asked me if I was ready for lunch.

"What are you fussing about lunch for. We could make good money with the time this crosscut's going to save us."

"Angelina and Alice brought up some of that tater salad and are cooking up some big, fat wieners on a barbeque. I guess Angelina was feeling a little guilty and got Alice out of bed so they could feed you guys. Angelina fed Smokey, Victor, and Cecil this morning… Said you guys need to keep your strength up."

"I can't get that Doney to drop. I guess I'll just drive a bolt through it. That ought to do it… A hot sit-down lunch you say…with tater salad?… Tell Angelina I'm sorry, but I'm going to stay with this."

That rock came down all right enough. I felt a little whiff of air on the back of my neck, my hard hat tilted back, then the Drill shut down and the leg collapsed. When I turned around to see what was going on I tripped over that chunk of rock. It was about five hundred pounds of rock, shaped like an inverted ice cream cone, that fell on the air-hose and shut the Jackleg down.

"Well, I see you've solved that rock problem." That was Timothy O'Leary as he walked by with his transit over his shoulder to map the Face and survey in the next day's line and grade.

This from an interview conducted by William C. Haight with a gentleman named Joe Strangle for the Federal Writers Project. (1939)

"One time when I was workin' on the high car near the head, I slipped and fell off. I was one of the very few men that ever got up and walked away from such an accident.

Another time a fellow was working on the arches near the segment. A big rock looked kinda loose, so he used a pick on it to see how tight she held. Well, the rock came out and covered him with a good many ton of rock. That feller was lucky: two planks fell across him in such a manner that the rock didn't crush him."

"He is the stone that makes people stumble, the rock that makes them fall. They stumble because they do not obey God's word, and so they meet the fate that was planned for them." That is what the Reverend said.

I was mounting the steps to Smokey and Angelina's veranda when he said it. It was then I began to get the uneasy feeling that I was to be the subject of Reverend Paulson's none-too-subtle oration that eve.

I was also served a burned wiener on day old bread for my Sunday night repast while the rest dined on leggy chicken steeped in homemade noodles with loganberry wine.

I would suppose the reason being Angelina didn't like to waste food.

There was Ragshag Bill from Buffalo,
I never will forget
He would roar all day and he'd roar all night
and I guess he's roaring yet
One day he fell in a prospect hole, in a roaring bad design
And in that hole he roared out his soul, in the days of '49
In the days of old, in the days of gold
How oft'times I repine for the days of old
When we dug up the gold,
in the days of '49.

The Days of Forty-Nine (Traditional American Folk Song)

209

Nora and Adeline

I didn't know Nora and Adeline Holleman. It seems like I would have seen them at one time or another. Granite was on the small side of small and I was in attendance at many of those social gatherings at the Granite Store, probably all of them in 1978 and 1979. Maybe I just assumed that all citizens of Granite were in attendance and they weren't. If Nora and Adeline were at any of those gatherings I'm not able get those names matched with any of the faces.

Adeline played that Hammond organ quite well, or so the citizenry of Granite at that time say. Some also say she had a beautiful voice. I wonder if that organ and that voice would have been heard drifting through the streets of Granite as the sun inched its way down behind Bolder Butte to the west.

As we rode out to Fennario
As we rode out to Fennario
Our captain fell in love with a lady like a dove
And he called her by name pretty Peggy-O
Will you marry me, pretty Peggy-O
Will you marry me, pretty Peggy-O

If you will marry me, I will set your cities free
And free all the ladies in the area-O
I would marry you, sweet William-O
I would marry you, sweet William-O
I would marry you, but your guineas are too few

And I fear my mama would be angry-O
What would your mama think, pretty Peggy-O
What would your mama think, pretty Peggy-O

(Scottish Folk Song)

Some say Adeline was born in the town of Siletz over on the Oregon coast in about 1917. Siletz was probably a town of about six hundred and seventy-five located on the remains of the Siletz Indian reservation at the time. That reservation would still have been a fairly good size place, and I'll wager the population of Siletz proper at that time would have been better than half Native American.

During the mid to late eighteen hundreds many a settler and his family traveled to that part of the world. If victuals weren't the most important thing on a settler's mind at the time they were very, very close, and farmland was becoming available as big pieces of the original Siletz reservation were being opened up to homesteading in a labyrinth of legislation, paperwork, and dollar exchange, that the native population, of that particular time and place, had little understanding.

Adeline spent her formative years in Yamhill, off that reservation, but not by much. A man named Loran Hoffman and his wife Ella were her parents. Loran was a Ledgman and a quarry worker there. He also listed as his profession, in the 1930 census, "Assembly of God." At that time a fervent denomination that spoke in tongues and believed in divine healing.

Loran was born in 1877, in that part of Oregon. He was the middle child in a family of six and he

211

completed eight years of schooling by the time he was eighteen years old. Many at that time knew how to read and write, but there were also many who didn't.

Ella was born in Iowa in 1887, the oldest in a family of eight. Her parents were both from Germany when they settled there. She knew how to read and write quite well. I would suppose her parents saw to it that she did, for she quite probably had to act as secretary, liaison, and interpreter, in many instances.

Loran met and married Ella in a place called Nez Perce, Idaho, in 1910.

Evidently Loran had two children by a previous companion, one born in 1905 and the other born in 1907, but when Adeline was born in 1917 she was listed as an only child.

Edward A. Morrow was born in 1929, somewhere in Yamhill County over in western Oregon. Probably in the very same hospital that Adeline Hoffman was born better than ten years earlier. His father, Bernard, and his mother, Mary, were living with his grandfather Gary (Guy) Allen at the time. Adeline Hoffman would have been about twelve years old and a resident of Nehalem at the time.

Adeline married a man named Clyde C Hollemon in 1935. Adeline was eighteen years old. Clyde was twenty.

Adeline Hollemon had her first child, a boy child she named Raymond in 1937. She graduated from Clinton Kelly High School of Commerce located in

Portland in 1941, the same year that World War II became official. Her name was in the yearbook for that year. She would have been twenty-four years old at the time, and that leads me to wonder where Clyde and Raymond spent their time. Then, in 1942, she birthed Nora.

Edward (Bud) Morrow's father left Bud and his mother in about 1935. The same year that Adeline Hoffman married Clyde C. Hollemon and became the Adeline Hollemon who would become Marshal Bud Morrow's neighbor and implacable enemy in a ghost town called Granite Oregon, thirty-seven years later.

Bud's grandfather was a part-time citizen of Granite Oregon in the nineteen forties. Granite's population would have been about ninety at that time. Bud would have been about eleven, and what there was of Bud's education was there, and in Baker City. I have even heard it said that Bud hadn't completed more than two years of schooling.

Adeline divorced Clyde Hollemon in 1966.

"That man I married!" Is the way Adeline referred to Clyde during the divorce proceedings. Part of that divorce may have had to do with the way Clyde treated Nora, always chiding her about being chubby and out of place.

Bud was first married when he was twenty-one years old. The year was 1950, and the bride's name was Loretta.

Loretta's parents probably had to travel the sixty miles through the winter's snows from Granite to the county seat down in Canyon City to get that done, for Loretta was only fifteen years old. It sounds rather out of place by today's standards, but it also needs to be understood that there were only six years between Bud and Loretta, and it was the year 1950, somewhere back in those craggy mountains of Eastern Oregon, and I would suppose that Loretta's parents welcomed one less mouth to feed.

Bud and Loretta were divorced seven months later.

This from an interview conducted by William C. Haight with Mrs. Neil Niven for the Federal Writers Project in 1939. Mrs. Niven was an eighteen-year-old citizen of Granite, in 1880 or so.

Spring! A young man's fancy lightly turns to thoughts o' love," might be true in parts of the world but not in Granite. There the young man's fancy and brawn were turned to avoiding landslides, digging out of the knee-deep mud, and damning up the swollen streams. The spring freshets would seep through the timbers of the mines, making them unsafe.

Work! Work! Work! That's what spring meant. However, gold was the Eldorado and mud and landslides were part of the price for the right to gamble for high-grade.

Marshal Bud had refurbished – or rather rebuilt – his grandfather's cabin, after he moved to Granite fulltime in 1966 due to a leg injury that preempted his employment opportunities elsewhere.

That cabin was not forty yards across Granite's main street from the place where Adeline and Nora would eventually dwell.

I guess you could say Bud was a part of Granite and had always been. He had seen Granite go from a population of near sixty in the forties to less than four in the sixties, and he was the Marshal Bud I got to know in 1977.

March 6th, 1982

*I*n the year 1972 Adeline moved to Granite Oregon; to that cabin she and Clyde had bought during more prosperous times. The money from that divorce not totally gone, but what was left had to last a while.

Nora, Adeline's daughter, had been alone all her life. I heard it said that when she was in her earlier years she cussed, chewed tobacco, and wore a pistol on her hip. Then again, I also heard it said that she was a good and pleasant person at the nursing profession down in Baker City. Then again some said just the opposite. Nora moved in with her mother in 1974, or around in there somewhere.

That cabin, Adeline and Nora's ramshackle home, was just across the road from Marshal Bud Morrow who was also the Mayor and head of the city council at the time.

I do not know what the rub was that brought about such a high state of antipathy towards Marshal Bud from those two. I think a good portion of that antipathy evolved around Marshal Bud's position as mayor, and the fact that Adeline and Nora did not think Bud was intelligent enough to hold such a position. Other than that no one seems to really have a good solid grip on the why and the wherefore of all that antipathy, it just was.

One incident that may have precipitated a lot of that hostility centered around the fact that a couple of bull elk got into a mating squabble and ended up dead in the Granite City water supply.

A town meeting was held to figure out what to do, and it was decided that about twenty-five hundred dollars would be needed for remedial repairs and a fence, but the town of Granite did not have much money, remedial or otherwise, so an emissary was sent to the county seat in Canyon City to find out how to tax the lots in Granite.

Adeline and Nora were quite vociferous in opposition to that tax, and any other monetary increases the city council of Granite deemed necessary. Probably because the monies coming in for them were minimal, providing for the necessities, beer every so often, and not much else. I would suppose that they could pay the power bill and heat that cabin while any other increases in expenditure would impose greater hardship.

Then there was the time that the city council of Granite decided it wouldn't be a good idea to be shooting pistols at squirrels in the city limits anymore and passed an ordinance accordingly.

Adeline and Nora took that bit of legislation quite personal and got quite loud about it.

It was then Marshal Bud began moving those council meetings to different locations so that Adeline and Nora wouldn't have to be dealt with.

Some say Adeline was very intelligent and colorfully expressive, and I guess that was the generally accepted state of things. So was the fact that both Adeline and Nora regarded Marshal Bud as: "That illiterate son of a bitch isn't smart enough to be mayor."

The Marshal and those two had to have known each other quite well. After all, they had lived in a place called Granite Oregon, just across the road from each other for nearly ten years. They may have known each other even before that.

They were citizens of Granite Oregon and they knew the same people.

Nora was bridesmaid at Bud's last wedding in 1976.

It was on that day Bud married Becky Ann McCracken who was eighteen years old. Bud was forty-six. I don't think that marriage lasted even a day. I heard it said that the morning after the nuptials Becky collected a six-pack of beer out of the refrigerator and went across Granite's main street to Adeline and Nora's and stayed with them for several days.

Maybe insanity in a cloistered environment doesn't take long to germinate. I would suppose that if you have little to occupy the mind the little issues in life will ferment, stew, and simmer into something that seems a whole lot bigger. Or maybe it was an insanity leftover from an earlier time. Then again maybe those insanities got mixed together and things just boiled over. That is about the only way I can get my head wrapped around what happened.

March 6th, 1982. That was the day Marshal Bud Morrow was found murdered on the floor of his cabin by a friend who was wondering why he had not seen the Marshal around.

The generally accepted theory is that Bud heard a knock on his door late on a Saturday night, and when he opened that door he was shot.

218

Nora and Adeline had a big, road-wise, drifter living with them by the name of Pasquale D'Onofrio at that time. Pat had found his way to Granite quite by accident not a week before.

Mr. D'Onofrio had a police record quite impressive. Pasquale was convinced he was an outlaw of the first degree, and I presume that is exactly what he was. He had been shot while escaping police in Connecticut and he had handcuff keys hidden in the lining of his leather jacket.

Nora and Pasquale had found one another, formed a relationship of sorts, and got good and drunk down at the Elkhorn Saloon in Sumpter the night of Marshal Bud's untimely demise. While there they made some quite incriminating comments. One of those comments, made by Pasquale, and heard by several of the bar's patrons. Something about being a hit man for the mob and Marshal Bud Morrow was in the way.

Most folks in Granite figured it was D'Onofrio who fired that fatal round, but he was the one to receive the least time in jail.

D'Onofrio received ten to twenty years in the state penitentiary.

When all was said and done, Nora went to jail for life plus twenty.

However, Adeline's trial was postponed due to the fact that she was considered quite insane. After psychiatric evaluation she was said to be paranoid and delusional, so the court said it was Ok to send her to the insane asylum for a time.

I have a cousin that was working for one of Adeline's court-appointed attorneys at the time. She said that Adeline had a "Few screws loose." Later she said that Adeline was "Either crazy or crafty."

The personnel down at the Oregon State Mental Institution in Salem could see no harm and gave that little old lady a pass to go downtown unsupervised, and she never returned.

Adeline spent better than two months on Oregon State's most wanted list before the police found her at a bed and breakfast in downtown Anchorage Alaska.

Adeline was eventually judged sane enough to stand trial and was sentenced to life in prison. I heard somewhere that she was paroled after ten years. That would have made her seventy-four years old when she got out in 1992.

Initially, my personal reaction to Bud's murder was a confused "What? Why?" Later, when all was condensed into the semblance of a semi-understandable happening, my response has accepted the "What." It did happen. It is that "Why" thing that gets to me the most.

Grays West and Company

Bud's funeral was held at Grays West and Company Funeral Home down there in Baker City, and it seemed there were quite a number of folks who came to the Marshal's funeral just to say they'd been there. I think I even saw Annalee Rice, the woman from KOIN TV that interviewed the Marshal back in the summer of 1978, standing in the doorway.

Apparently, Bud was a bit of a celebrity in that part of the world at that time

People were backed out the door of that funeral home and out into the yard. There were people I knew out in the streets and hanging around their pickups that could not get inside.

There were many faces I had seen before. Some I had grown up with. This was Baker and this was where I came from. I also noticed many faces I did not know

I had always assumed that Granite was the Marshal's family, if I had ever considered Bud as having a family at all. I had never even thought about Bud having a genetic family. I was wondering then who they were and where they came from.

I didn't particularly want to crowd in amongst those already crowded in. I didn't even want to crowd in amongst those on the porch and on the stairs. I was going to content myself to sit under the shade of those big trees and listen to the unintelligible drone of Buds service from outside in the fresh air.

Katy Gunn was leaning up against one of those big Maples out there in Grays West and Company's lawn smoking a cigarette. She wasn't dressed much different than usual; still in jeans and a western plaid shirt with snap pockets. She opened one of those pockets and proffered me a smoke as I approached. We leaned against that tree and half listened to Bud's eulogy, and the birds in those trees.

I had earned my credentials, so to speak. I was now officially a tramp miner. (*A distinction I later learned to curse*) I had been following the work around.

Granite was home base those first two summers, and those first three winters. It was the beginning of that third summer things changed for Cecil, Terry, Timothy O'Leary, and I.

We three had been selected, quite probably because George assumed we would not mind spending a little time in the middle of the sage, dust, and rattlesnakes. That and the fact that we carried no marital baggage that would also need to shuffled around and moved.

We had been south of Winnemucca Nevada working a narrow vein out close to the Black Rock for nearly a year and a half. We were working for a man named Toney Luzuriaga, the owner of the Gem Bar there in Winnemucca at the time. A Basque gentleman that had probably learned the most profane words in the American language before anything else.

South Mountain, up in Idaho, was waiting for us when we finished that little job: Cecil, Timothy O'Leary, and I. We didn't even have to find our way back to Granite.

Instead of making that left to stay on Interstate Highway 95 and the asphalt as it headed north out of Jordan Valley it was straight ahead. Then it was follow those rough wooden signs George had nailed to a Juniper at each fork in the road. Those rough wooden signs that had "South Mountain Mine" stenciled in white, underlined with a white arrow pointing the way.

It was Katy Gunn that told me what had happened to Marshal Bud.

She was bringing a load of timber to South Mountain from Sonny's mill at the Cougar when the truck she was driving blew a tire. When that tire was repaired she decided to spend the night at Jim Zatica's motel down there in Jordan Valley. When she phoned into the Cougar from that pay phone sitting next to Zatica's Texaco the next morning George told her the Marshal was found shot to death in his cabin.

Those of us at South Mountain were nearly all from Granite, or Sumpter, or Baker, and all of us knew the Marshal quite well.

Katy told me, and I guess she figured I was the one who was going to tell those that knew him.

I never was, and probably never will be, much good at that sort of thing.

I walked into the shop where Thor was rebuilding that mucker that never really ran the same after Katy Gunn had submerged it a couple of years before. I told him first because he was the one that probably knew Bud the longest. He looked at me with a blank expression, then his eyes clouded over a little bit. Then he shook his head and bent back to his work, as if he did not want to deal with what he had just heard until his shift was over.

It was obvious Buds funeral had affected Katy Gunn rather deeply. She kept her eyes out the window on the passenger's side as we joined the procession behind that long black hearse from Grays West and Funeral Parlor. That long black hearse covering all that followed with a layer of dust from that dusty road we used to call the North Fork Highway
Katy slumped back into the seat and plugged a cassette tape she had in her pocket into my new pickups tape player as we were following the funeral procession up to the Granite Cemetery. Why Katy chose that song I do not know. That tune sticks in my head to this day. I don't know why. It just does.

Oh, the lights of Magdala flicker
Dimly on the shore.
Holy sailor sailing on the sea
Patiently waiting she walked quietly
To the door
Another lonely night in Galilee

Magdalene, don't wrap your dreams in sorrow
Save them for tomorrow if it comes
When we'll meet within the circle
Round the sun

224

Oh, if heaven were a lady don't you
Know you'd been the one

Kris Kristofferson – Spooky Ladies Sideshow
(1972)

They, whoever they were, had arranged that the deputies from around the two counties of Baker and Grant give the Marshal a twenty-one-gun salute as he was being laid to rest.

There were seven deputies in all, and they were going to fire twenty-one rounds with their pistols, but I don't think they had considered the fact that they might need some blank cartridges, or whoever was supposed to bring them forgot. I saw them look at each other with concerned expressions on their faces, and then I saw them go into a huddle. I guess they decided to go ahead and use live rounds and just fire up and away.

Those shots were never really synchronized. There would be six pistols fired and then the one on the end, then the one on the end and then another and then the rest. The third volley sounded like a loud string of firecrackers going off.

I don't know what the Marshal would have thought about his funeral. I think he would have been a little surprised at the turnout. I do know that all of us that knew him as Marshal Bud were. Katy and I just stood on the sidelines with Smokey, Angelina, Timothy O'Leary, Cecil, Jim, Alice, Sonny, Thor and the rest. We watched as he was lowered and covered with that rocky soil.

I think Bud was the last person buried in the Granite Cemetery. I do not know that for a fact, but I do know that people could not be buried just anywhere they chose in 1982. I think the powers that be made an exception in the Marshal's case. Probably because he belonged there. It seemed natural and proper.

After Bud's Funeral

Sonny and Thor were leaning on their elbows with their backs against the bar of the Granite Store after Bud's funeral wound down and most of those that did not live in Granite proper were gone. Smokey and Angelina were at a table towards to back.

They were listening to seemingly adolescent men and women talking about the time that Katy Gunn had driven that mucker under about ten feet of water and nearly drown... laughing.

"And there was the time you shot out all that timber and made it hard for me to get the down payment together for a new car." Katy addressed that remark in my direction.

"One thing I'll say is that you got a lot of mileage out of that old Plymouth before you drove it down the Slot and got it beat up a little more." Timothy O'Leary said as he pointed his finger a Katy with a smile on his face.

Katy Gunn's gloom was dissipating with the conviviality and cold beer.

We'd been pretty much part of each other's lives for nearly four years. We'd worked together, lived under the same roof, and eaten each other's breakfast. We knew each other as well as anyone could, I suppose. We'd seen each other naked, and we knew each other's scars, both physical and otherwise.

We were comrades now. We'd heaved heavy timber and fought clay dikes. We'd busted and skinned our knuckles and noses. We'd quite truly

227

learned the value of hot water, good food, and the absolute wonderfulness of a warm fire after the knuckle busting labor was done.

We were talking about the first time we lost the face. We were talking about the time the Marshal got us out of the hole in the dark of the night to get Harley's truck out of Granite Creek.

We were talking about the time Terry had performed a chivalrous act at Cattle Kates, and how Katy dealt with Alfonzo.

Marlene, Victors wife, was sitting on the porch of the Granite Store watching Billy Shortstack teach Little Lola, who was now six, to throw rocks at a squirrel sitting on a stump across the road when Sonny went out to his truck and brought in a jug of that Virginia made moonshine and passed it around to those so inclined. That was against the law I'm quite sure, but Lance didn't seem to care. Who was around to catch us, anyway?

Marshal Bud didn't even seem to be concerned when he was around… which he wasn't anymore. He was gone and that fact left something kind of unhooked; something that wouldn't quite get settled down; something that would creep into the back of the mind and leave a little darkness behind.

There was a tune on Willies Juke Box that a lot of us liked. Cecil put in quarter and "Who'll Stop the Rain," took hold about the same time as Sonny's moonshine.

As long as I remember
The rain's been comin down

228

Clouds of mystery pourin'
Confusion on the ground.
Good men through the ages
Tryin' to find the sun
And I wonder, still I wonder
Who'll stop the rain?

I went down Virginia
Seekin' shelter from the storm
Caught up in the fable
I watched the tower grow.
Five-year plans and new deals
Wrapped in golden chains
And I wonder, still I wonder
Who'll stop the rain?

John Fogerty (1970)

It was then I grabbed Katy Gunn and we began to swing around where there was room, and Jim and Alice soon joined in. Billy Shortstack heard the Willie's Jukebox and the dancing, came in from outside, grabbed her daddy's hand, and they started to dance. Clogging is what they called it back there in Virginia; clogging to a drifting middle beat tune. It seemed to fit, in that place, at that time.

There was a part to Sonny and Billy's dance that put the heel of the right foot down on the floor with a little bit of a thump. And soon Sonny's heel hit a little harder. And then Sonny let it go. And then we all let it go. Sonny's heel would come down and then bottles were banged on the tables and the bar. And then all those boots would crash on the floor in time to the music. The Marshal was gone and there wasn't much else could be done about that but get angry, and I guess that's what we did.

Trampin Out

I think all of us would have liked things to stay the way they were a little longer, but we could also see it wasn't going to be. The Marshal was gone and soon the Cougar.

We could divine that the Cougar was getting short and would not be there much longer. We could see it. We just didn't talk about it.

The ore body was nearly blocked out and ready to mine, but the investors had already been stoped-out and didn't want to go much further. Those that put up the money had decided that enough of that money had been spent so why spend any more.

Some of us had already tramped out. I was already at South Mountain and never really got back to Granite other than Bud's funeral and just travel through.

I would see Cecil down in Baker when I got back on days off. We'd share a beer down at Cattle Kate's and talk, but eventually I didn't see him anymore. I heard that he had hooked up at the Iron Dike down on the Snake River.

Cecil would have liked that; being down on the Snake River. What happened to him after the Iron Dike shut down, I don't know: probably drifting; probably wandering.

I never saw Katy Gunn again after Bud's funeral. I was headed back to South Mountain when I saw her waving that final goodbye from Smokey and Angelina's porch down there in Dog Patch

A few days later George called me from his office up at the Cougar and told me that the load of timber was going to be a day or so late. He said that Katy said she needed to take care of a few things back in Frisco. He also said he'd seen her driving down the North Fork Highway the next day with what looked like everything she owned stuffed in or tied on to that little pickup truck she then drove.

In 1984 I received a letter from Timothy O'Leary at a general delivery address in Winnemucca Nevada. He said that he and Katy had teamed up down in San Francisco about a year after the Cougar was shut down. (*I figured that might happen, sooner or later.*)

Timothy said Katy had gotten back in her son Christopher's life, and he and Katy had been there when Christopher graduated from high school. He said that Katy had given Christopher the nearly five-thousand dollars that she had saved up while living in Granite and working at the Cougar for a graduation present.

Then Timothy told me that he, Katy Gunn, and Christopher were working a gold mine in a place called Broad Pass, somewhere east of Anchorage up in Alaska.

Go figure.

It was also in 1984 that I saw Smokey's obituary in the Record Courier. He would have been near seventy years old by that time. I do not remember the exact words in that obit.

I remember this:

We'll hear no more

that lilting fiddle's tune
Drifting
Through that little
Rusty Town

And I would wager Angelina had a strong hand in the writing of it.

Smokey had managed to get his leg pinched between a truck and a mucker and had to spend some time in the Hospital. While there he was diagnosed with the cancer.

Angelina said that he had known it all along but did not want to admit it.

I also heard that Angelina had joined the church, referring to the Mormon Church down in the valley. I guess she figured the Mormon Church was a bit more stable than the Reverend Paulson's "Church of the Guiding Light."

The Reverend? I often wonder if he's the vicar of the "Church of Guiding Light", that congregation that had found its way into that converted pizza parlor down on Tenth Street in Baker City. He'd be eighty-three years old right now.

I heard that Sonny was in Ironside building wooden boxes for the orchards over in the Treasure Valley after the Cougar shut off its pumps and closed its portals.

Victor, Marlene and Little Lola probably moved back to what was originally their home in the Blue Ridge Mountains in Virginia. I think Marlene was always a little homesick for "Back Home "and there was little to hold them to Granite and the life they had made there.

I heard that Jim and Alice married, had two children, and were working what was left of the oil boom in Gillette Wyoming in 1990.

Harley? After all the little mines in that part of the world went the same way as the Cougar he had to do something, so he took up the task of cutting firewood for the folks in that part of the world that needed it.

Then he and Dar moved down to Sumpter, from what I hear. It's my understanding that Dar had managed to turn her hobby of bisque ware into a fairly profitable business of sorts, and they had to move to more civilized environs.

I even heard that Harley had become a rather social animal when he reached his late forties.

Go figure.

Thor stayed in Granite... it was his home. He probably stayed busy patching together old pickups and broken slushers. He started on the Oregon Coast, and Granite was where it was going to end for him. He would have been sixty-five years of age in 1984.

Terry and I were down in Northern Nevada about a year after South Mountain went away. When that little job finished we drifted apart. He went east and I went back to Baker City to try to make a little less of a "pick it up, pack it up, and move on" sort of life, without much success.

The Granite Store I knew back the late seventies and early eighties burned down under mysterious circumstances in 1983 or thereabouts. A more sophisticated store with a comfortable lodge for the bed and breakfast crowd now resides at the corner of what is now known as the Elkhorn Scenic Byway and Center Street.

Cattle Kate's is now known as the "Sports Bar," with a television in every corner and a basketball hoop standing at the end of what used to be the dance floor. The crowd is pretty much the same though. Same age as us back then. Probably the same in a lot of ways.

Dog Patch is gone.
Celeste, my wife of better than thirty years, and I drove by there in 2009, taking the backroad to a nephew's wedding in Ukiah. We were going that direction because I wanted to reminisce about a past life. Something Celeste can sometimes be tolerant of…. Sometimes not.
That flat piece of ground on which Dog Patch sat down by Granite Creek is empty. Not even the river-stone foundations remain.
A man – I should know, never knew, or don't remember – that has lived in that part of the world for fifty years said that it was on federal land and the Forest Service came in one day and it was gone.

I guess that's just the way we were, back then. Back when we were a lot younger. When life seemed a lot different. Life before mortgages, car payments and the 401K. Back when we were a piece of a seemingly rootless generation, looking for job, a paycheck, a roof... and a tune. That's the way we were.

Don't look back
A new day is breakin'
It's been too long since I felt this way
I don't mind where I get taken
The road is callin'
Today is the day I can see
It took so long to realize I'm much too strong
Not to compromise
Now I see what I am is holding me down
I'll turn it around
I finally see the dawn arrivin'
I see beyond the road I'm drivin'
Far away and left behind

Tom Scholz (1978)

The End

Or, as Timothy O'Leary might say in his often-annoying Spanish

"Hacia Adelante"

CPSIA information can be obtained
at www.ICGtesting.com
Printed in the USA
BVHW081004270522
638205BV00031B/703